400 DAYS OF OPPRESSION

WRATH JAMES WHITE

BLOOD BOUND BOOKS

ISBN 978-1-940250-02-1

Artwork by Alex McVey

Printed in the United States of America

First Edition

Visit us on the web at:
www.bloodboundbooks.net

Also from Blood Bound Books:

Habeas Corpse by Nikki Hopeman

Loveless by Dev Jarrett

The Sinner by K. Trap Jones

Mother's Boys by Daniel I. Russell

Knuckle Supper by Drew Stepek

Sons of the Pope by Daniel O'Connor

Dolls by KJ Moore

At the End of All Things by Stony Graves

The Return by David A Riley

To Mom

PROLOGUE

⁊⹁

It was the last day of school. The bell rang, signaling the end of another grade and the beginning of three joyous months of summer. Kids flooded from the old, red-brick middle school building like a swarm of ants from a poisoned nest. Smiles were the dominant expression but not the only ones. There were fights, kids making the most of their last opportunity to settle year-long scores, the haunted expressions of those who had received bad report cards and were terrified at the thought of what their parents would do to them when they got home. A mix of emotions from outrage to apathy painted the features of the students who'd learned they needed to attend summer school to complete the grade and those who learned they would not graduate to the next grade no matter what they did.

Notes were passed and dates were hurriedly made. Girls and boys exchanged phone numbers, promising to stay in touch over the summer. There were a few tearful goodbyes from kids who had graduated and were moving on to different high schools. Kenyatta was one of the latter. He turned fourteen this year. He would be entering the ninth grade at Creative and Performing Arts High School in the fall. This was his last chance to tell Christie how he felt about her or he would likely never see her again.

Kenyatta was in love. His teenage hormones and emotions were a raging wildfire within him. He felt like he was losing his mind. He'd been walking Christie home from school each day for the last six or seven weeks. Ever since he found out she'd told someone that, if she ever dated a black boy, it would be him. He'd been deeply flattered, but it was more than that. He was interested and soon that interest became an obsession.

Christie was pretty, adorable, so different from the hardened hoochies in his neighborhood. She was quiet and shy. All the girls he'd grown up with were loud and obnoxious in comparison. She didn't wear gold chains or big earrings with her name on them. There were no designer labels on her clothes. She was simple, sweet, more like the girls he saw on television who were so innocent and...white. He couldn't help wondering if he was obsessing over her solely because of the color of her skin. That's what his mother and his aunts would think. They hated the idea of white bitches taking all the good black men. Was his affection for Christie a reflection of his own self-hatred? He didn't know. All he knew was ever since he'd found out she was interested in him, he wasn't interested in anyone else.

Kenyatta was one of the most popular kids in school. He was the president of the student council, an honor roll student, and he was captain of the basketball team. He'd dated the most popular girls in school. There wasn't a black girl in Taft Junior High who wouldn't have fallen all over themselves to date him and many of them were much sexier than Christie. But none of them had made him feel like this before. She liked to read as much as he did, geeked out as much over the release of the next Stephen King novel as he did, loved Prince and

Stevie Wonder and poetry and trips to the art museum and picnics. She was romantic and so he didn't feel like an idiot thinking romantic thoughts about her. He had never considered dating a white girl before. Not that he was ever opposed to it or saw anything wrong with it. He had just never entertained the thought in the past. It had never occurred to him as an option. As much as the world had changed in 1995 compared to when his mom was in high school, during the height of the civil rights movement, it hadn't changed that much in Philadelphia. The racial divides were now marked by street signs. On one side of Frankford Avenue, there were projects filled with blacks and Puerto Ricans. On the other side, were poor whites and farther down Frankford Avenue were middle and upper-middle class whites. This area was less a melting pot than an arena with teams marked by their accents and skin color.

Back then, all of Philadelphia was similarly divided. WASPS in Northeast Philadelphia. Italians and Jews in South Philly. Irish in Frankford and Fishtown. Blacks and Puerto Ricans in North and West Philadelphia. Taft Junior High was located right on the border between a black and Puerto Rican neighborhood and a middle-class white neighborhood. They all went to the same school, played on the same teams, hung out together at school. But after school, they went their separate ways. Even in the 90s, interracial relationships in Philadelphia were rare.

Kenyatta thought the young Italian girl was the most beautiful creature he'd ever seen. He couldn't stop thinking about her and he knew she felt the same way about him. He could see it in her eyes when they hugged before parting ways at Frankford Avenue each afternoon, just on the edge of her neighborhood. This wasn't just a casual friendship. She was into him. Today was the last day of school and Kenyatta knew he had to say something to her, had to tell her how he felt about her.

There was a knot in his throat as Kenyatta walked up the long hill with Christie. He reached out and took Christie's hand and she gave it a squeeze, smiling awkwardly at him. They walked the rest of the way, holding hands and talking about what she was going to do over the summer, how he would get along in the new school, if he would come back to visit all his friends at Taft. Kenyatta could barely complete a thought. His mind was preoccupied by the stop sign ahead. That was where they normally hugged and said goodbye. Only, today, it would be for the last time.

"What are you thinking about?" she asked, smiling up at him with those deep dimples that looked like you could fall into them and those gray and green eyes with the halo of brown around the irises like the mouth of a volcano. A lump formed in Kenyatta's throat and he swallowed it down. His leg was trembling.

"Uh. Um. I was just thinking about you."

"I'm gonna miss you," Christie said, still smiling at him, batting her long eyelashes without the slightest clue what she was doing to him.

"I love you." The words just slipped out. There was a shocked expression on Christie's face and Kenyatta did something else he hadn't exactly been planning to

4

do. He kissed her before she could answer. When their lips met, Kenyatta's pulse skyrocketed. He was waiting to see if she'd return the kiss, push him away and slap him, scream 'rape.' He didn't know what to expect. When he felt her hands on the back of his head, her lips part and her tongue dart out to meet his, every muscle in his body felt like it suddenly lost cohesion. He felt like he had no weight, as if he would float right off the sidewalk or be inhaled into Christie's lungs with her next breath. Then, abruptly, she broke off the kiss. There were tears in her eyes when she looked at him. She said goodbye then ran to the corner across Frankford Avenue and out of his life. The pain in his chest was worse than what he felt when his grandpa died, worse than when his dog, Prince, ran away. This felt like a mortal wound, something he would never recover from. He stared after her with his mouth hanging open, the feel of her lips still burning on his, the taste of her mouth haunting his tongue. He turned and walked back down the hill toward home.

Kenyatta didn't leave his bedroom when his mom came home that night. He sat in the room in the dark. He didn't come down for dinner, didn't watch TV. He just sat there, thinking about Christie and fighting back the tears. If he allowed himself to cry, he wasn't sure he'd ever stop. When his mother knocked on his door, poked her head into his room, and asked him if he was okay, he lost the battle with his emotions and the tears rained from his eyes like a storm.

"Oh, baby, what's wrong?"

He couldn't stop the sobbing long enough to reply. His mother held him in her arms, rocking him the way she had when he was a baby, until the last tears had fallen.

"I'm never going to see Christie again. I love her, Ma."

His mother gave him one of those wise, knowing smiles, a smile that said: "You should have asked me all along. I've got the answer right here."

"Why don't you just call her?"

And so he did.

"Christie?"

"Kenyatta?"

"Yeah, it's me. Why did you run away?"

"I was scared—I mean hurt. Why did you kiss me like that? Why'd you tell me you love me? I was already missing you. That was just mean. Now I'm never going to see you again."

"It doesn't have to be like that. We can still see each other. You can be my girlfriend. I'll come see you every day."

There was a long silence on the other end of the phone.

"My parents would kill me. They don't believe in that."

They don't believe in that.

There was no need to say what "*that*" was. They both knew. Black boys dating white girls. Race-mixing. Miscegenation.

"But..." Kenyatta didn't know what to say.

"Good bye, Kenyatta." She was crying now. "I'll miss you."

"I-I love you, Christie." This time it sounded like a plea, which it was. He couldn't believe that this was the end of it.

"I love you too, Kenyatta."

"Then—"

The phone went dead. She had hung up. Kenyatta was stunned, broken. It was the first time he'd ever been in love and he didn't know what he was supposed to do with this pain. It hurt so bad it felt like his mind was going to shatter into a million little jagged pieces. He stood up and left his room. He passed his mom in the kitchen.

"How'd it go?"

He didn't answer. He just walked out the door. He walked all the way to Frankford Avenue and crossed it. An hour later. He walked back home, ran up to his room, undressed, and jumped into the shower. After his shower, he took his clothes down to the dumpster and threw them in the trash. He came back upstairs, passing his mother again who was looking at him with concern.

"You okay, Kenyatta?"

"I'm fine."

"You want something to eat?"

"I'm not hungry."

"How did it go with your little girlfriend?"

He shook his head and closed his bedroom door. Kenyatta held the little scrap of paper he'd written Christie's address and phone number on in his hand. There was a dark stain on it and he smeared it with his thumb. She wasn't home when he had knocked on her door. Her mom and dad told him she had gone to a friend's house, staring at him with eyes full of suspicion. It was probably best she wasn't there. Maybe it wasn't. Maybe things would have gone differently if she'd been there. He didn't know. It was hard to resist the urge to call her, but he would wait. He would give her a few days to grieve before he reached out to her again.

CHAPTER I

My name is Natasha and I am a slave, property. I have been owned in one way or another for as long as I can remember. I was a slave to addictions, a slave to my past, a slave to my low expectations of men and even lower expectations of myself. Now, I have stripped away all the pretensions. No more self-deception. The bonds are as real as the need for them. They are honesty, truth, making the metaphor concrete and there is freedom in this, in the spirit if not the flesh.

My master's name is Kenyatta and I love him. I love him with all my heart, more than my own pride and self-respect, more than all the pain and humiliation. More than the discomfort and inconvenience. I love him and I want to marry him some day, some day soon, and that's what made it all tolerable.

I panicked as my own humid breath rebounded off the inside of the coffin lid. The press of the pine box against my sides and the oppressive heat escalated my claustrophobia. I blinked the sweat from my eyes and coughed as I inhaled more of the hot moist air. It was hard to believe it contained any oxygen at all. The overwhelming heat, the smell of my own piss and shit coming from the bucket just yards away, was making it increasingly difficult to breathe. The nauseating fumes boiled in my lungs as I choked them down. I tried not to think about it, afraid that dwelling on the situation would bring on a panic attack. I was trying my best not to freak out.

All I had to do was say one word and my oppression would end. I would be free. I could go back to my own warm bed, back to eating regular food, taking regular showers and using the toilet whenever I wanted. All I had to do was say the safe word. But I couldn't. It just wasn't in me. No matter what, I just couldn't say that word.

I hugged my breasts as I began to sob, noting with some remorse that I had lost more weight and my breasts were at least a full cup size smaller. I was wasting away, slowly losing everything that made me attractive to him.

Long rivulets of perspiration and blood trailed down my forearms as I scratched obsessively at the lid of the coffin, wincing when my fingernails snapped, embedded in the wood, and splinters speared my cuticles. It had become almost a nervous habit now. I held no real hope of escaping.

The iron shackles dug deep into my collarbone, wrists, and ankles, weighing me down. The slightest movement tore open the slow-healing wounds where the metal had abraded my skin. Trickles of red stained my chest.

I wanted to get out, to just say fuck it all and end this stupid experiment. But I knew I would stay. I'd endure it all, no matter what he came up with, because I loved him.

I know that makes me sound pitiful, like one of those stupid trailer park whores who stay with men that get drunk and beat them every night, and yeah, I've been one of those stupid bitches before too, but this is different. Kenyatta loves me and I volunteered for this. It was what I wanted, what we needed. And ending the experiment would have meant ending our relationship.

The swaying coffin made me nauseous as I rocked back and forth, unhealed wounds scratching against the hard wood. The box was suspended three feet above the concrete floor by chains anchored at its center so that my slightest movement rocked to create the effect of a ship on rough waters. I shifted positions and sent the coffin tilting and reeling. I felt seasick. With great effort I resisted the urge to vomit up the crappy mess he'd been feeding me the last couple of days, choking it back down as the gorge rose in my throat. I was hungry and thirsty, and my bowels were full and threatening to fail. There was no way I could have imagined I'd be this miserable.

The pipes rattled above me as Kenyatta took his morning shower. I was jealous. I wanted a shower too. Even the horrific reek of my bucket/toilet wasn't strong enough to mask the stench of my own body odor. I smelled like sweat and vomit. I listened longingly to the shower, depressing myself even more. At least now I had some idea of the time. He would be coming to get me soon.

I shifted positions and sucked in a quick breath as a scab on my elbow scraped open against the rough wood. A door slammed above. Pots and pans rattled. The smell of frying bacon drifted down from the kitchen. My stomach roiled. I would have killed for some pancakes with butter and lots of syrup or an omelet with spinach and feta cheese like the kind he made for me the first night I spent at his house, when he woke me up the next morning with breakfast in bed and then fucked me hard on his satin-sheets before leaving for work and leaving me there alone to finish breakfast at my leisure. I had felt like a queen then. Today I just hoped he would remember to feed me.

I smelled the boiled yams that, along with the occasional pot of horse beans boiled to a mushy pulp, had become my regular source of sustenance. In my hunger, even this repulsive gruel sounded appealing. Even with my bowels threatening to give way, my hunger was winning out. At least it meant he had not forgotten me.

I took stock of myself, suddenly self-conscious and embarrassed, as I lay there quivering and sweating, struggling not to urinate in my little pine box. I felt disgusting. I didn't want Kenyatta to see me this way. I wished I were allowed to take a shower, curl my hair, put on some makeup and lingerie like I used to do when we had first started dating. I wanted to be pretty and clean for him.

I whimpered aloud when Kenyatta's footsteps descended the basement stairs. I felt like some ridiculously loyal dog, eagerly awaiting the return of the master who whipped and kicked it. The silly little bondage games I'd played with my past lovers had done nothing to prepare me for this. I'd been exploited and abused by men before. Anonymous men who didn't give a fuck about me. This was different. This was the man who was supposed to love me, the man I wanted to spend the rest of my life with. I was in way over my head, but it was too late. If I backed out now he'd never marry me.

"Oh God, baby, I can't take this! I'm freaking the fuck out! I feel like I'm going to throw up," I cried.

I strained against the lid of the casket, tears weeping from the corners of my eyes, hoping Kenyatta would hear me and hurry to my rescue. Hoping that if I sounded pitiful enough he wouldn't have the heart to continue this madness. The safe word went through my mind again and I toyed with it, wondering if I could say it. Wondering how bad things would have to get for that word to lose its repugnancy. I mouthed the word but refused to say it out loud, realizing with some dismay that I never could. Even though it was the only way my life would go back to normal, there was no way I was going to say that disgusting word. Just thinking it made me feel guilty. Of course Kenyatta knew from the start that I couldn't say it. That's why he had picked that particular word as our safe word. A word that stated quite clearly that I had rejected him. A word that would end our relationship forever. He knew that I'd die in that damned box before I'd say it.

When Kenyatta opened the lid of the coffin, I almost screamed. He stood there staring down at my nudity as I curled up, trying to hide my wretchedness from his eyes. I hated him seeing me like this. But that was the point, wasn't it? It was the only way I would ever understand.

He switched on the keyless light, little more than a bare light bulb attached to the trusses above our heads, and one hundred watts speared my retinas, unbearable after nearly ten hours of solid darkness. I recoiled from it, temporarily blinded, but more ashamed than anything. I knew how I must look to him, naked and unwashed. He continued to stare down at me as I squinted against the glare. He smiled and my heart felt suddenly lighter. Then his voice boomed, loud and stern.

"Come out of there. It's exercise time."

Oh God. How can I exercise with my bladder about to burst?

He sat my meal of boiled yams and rice down on a stool and picked up a small talking drum and a stick.

"Get out of there now! Dance!"

He began to pound the drum. If I didn't dance he would go for the whip soon. I had no choice but to obey. I crawled from my wooden casket and lowered myself unsteadily to the concrete floor. My stomach lurched as the casket wobbled and tilted, spilling me out. My legs shook and the room reeled as if everything were still swaying back and forth. I fought to maintain my balance and quiet the dizziness as I stood before him drenched in sweat and blood. Soon the room stopped swaying and the nausea in my stomach lulled into the dull ache of hunger.

I stared at the floor, afraid to meet his gaze, forbidden to, but wanting so much to see his beautiful face and finely chiseled body. Kenyatta was an impressive physical specimen, six foot six with thick striated muscles coiled like pistons beneath his ebon skin. His head and face were clean shaven, and smooth, and his strong jaw, high cheek bones, and intense black eyes gave him the look of African royalty. He was the very definition of manhood to me and I adored every inch of him as I had proven on many occasions, as I was proving now by enduring his terrible lesson.

I had lost a lot of weight in the week since my ordeal began. I knew that Kenyatta preferred me thicker. My hips were smaller now, my breasts and thighs not quite as heavy. My ass, which had been perfect for Kenyatta's tastes, had dwindled away to nothing and I was embarrassed as I stood before him. His body was still perfect.

I began to dance, trying to shut out my urgent need to pee. The drumbeat pounded through me as I gyrated my hips and stomped and wiggled and clapped. I was not a very good dancer and this was one of his favorite humiliations for me. Maybe if he had put on some country music. I knew how much Kenyatta hated country, but I could have done something with a little Toby Keith playing in the background. Maybe an old school two step and a twist. That drum playing alone like that was hard to get into, especially when I was hungry and needed to piss. Kenyatta called this exercise, but I knew it was just another way to further degrade me. I was grateful when he turned the hose on me.

"Keep dancing!"

I danced in the cool spray from the hose and I urinated freely, hoping the water would mask what I was doing. It didn't work. Kenyatta turned off the hose, stood, and slapped me to the floor. I know, I'm starting to sound like the abused trailer trash wife again. But I liked it when he slapped me...usually...when he did it during sex. But not today, when I looked like shit and I was all miserable and hungry.

"That's not sexy, Natasha. Now dance again without the water sports."

I started crying again. This was so much harder than I had ever imagined it would be and it had only been a week. One week of constant torture. One week of unending insanity. There were still three hundred and ninety-three days left to go in my lesson. I was tough. I could make it. My life had been hell since I could remember and I'd survived it. I'd survive this too.

I know men like Kenyatta...yeah...black men, think that pretty white girls like me have easy lives. But that's bullshit. My life ain't never been easy. I grew up poor. I grew up abused, and I've been abused by men in one way or another ever since the first time I let that Indian boy from the reservation fuck me in the back of his daddy's truck. I was twelve years old and it wasn't the first time I'd had sex, just the first time I'd consented to it. It didn't make it any better. He was no nicer to me than the others had been.

Kenyatta finished hosing me off and then I was ordered to stand there and drip dry. The chains were heavy. It made standing difficult, especially with all the weight I had lost on my diet of beans and yams. Despite the oppressive heat down there, I began to shiver. Finally, Kenyatta tossed the plate of food at my feet and watched as I greedily scarfed it up with my bare hands. He had reduced me to some undignified animal, but I could not hate him. I knew his people had suffered far worse at the hands of my ancestors. He was quick to remind me how much worse it would be if I were sharing my cramped quarters with six-hundred others, breathing, sweating, and defecating in the same dank humid air I was inhaling. Lying spooned together so tight that some suffocated from the sheer press of bodies and others died of dysentery and malaria. I knew he spared me these horrors out of no kindness on his part, but only due to the impracticality of trying to get another six-hundred slaves to willingly submit themselves to the ordeal I had volunteered myself for.

Ever since I started teaching English to seventh and eighth graders, I'd had to deal with Black History Month and every year I had made sure to avoid exposing my students to the horrors of the trans-Atlantic slave trade. I would skip past it as if it were a mere footnote in the history of black people and not the single most impactful moment in black history. I would avoid talking about the beatings, the hangings, the families separated and destroyed and just rush right into talking about Harriet Tubman and Frederick Douglas and then on to Dr. Martin Luther King Jr. Now, I wondered if I had been protecting the children or myself.

The food tasted like warm shit. I was so hungry it didn't matter. Besides, there was nothing I could do about it. I either ate this nasty crap or I starved. It wasn't like Kenyatta was going to make me steak and eggs. This is what the slaves had eaten, so this is what I would eat until Kenyatta decided otherwise.

I risked a glance up at him as I continued to scarf down my food. The look on his face could only be described as one of absolute disgust. There was something else there though. Pity? Sympathy? Sorrow? It was the look you gave to a crippled homeless person when he pissed himself. I just wasn't sure if it was for me or for his ancestors. I suspected it was a little of both. If I hadn't felt wretched and disgusting before, that look had solved that. I lowered my head back to my bowl, trying not to choke on my food as I began to sob again.

Knowing that I could end it at any time made it worse. All I had to do was say that horrible word and he'd immediately unchain me and set me free. Of course Kenyatta, being the type of man he is, made the safe word something as reprehensible as the treatment I was now being subjected to. To go free, all I would have to do is yell "Nigger." Not just say it. He didn't want me to whisper it apologetically. He'd made that clear. I had to yell it at the top of my lungs. He knew I'd never do that. That would only multiply my "whitey guilt" as Kenyatta called it. So instead I endured.

I hated Kenyatta standing above me with that look of pity and disgust twisting his features as I shoveled the mushy gruel into my face, kneeling on my hands and knees like an animal. I felt like some loathsome repugnant thing and I wondered if he still loved me after seeing me like this. I was afraid to ask, though I knew he would have answered me. I was afraid to hear the reply. Sometimes, on the days when the beatings were the most severe, he'd break character for a while and whisper to me that he still loved me and that he was proud of me for going through this for him. He'd hold me close to him as I wept and bled and swab my wounds with vinegar and alcohol before putting me back in my box. Both my love and my commitment renewed for a while, I'd lie in my box dreaming of being with him when this was all over. I'd imagine lying in bed with him, nestled against his powerful body, my head on his chest, listening to his heartbeat and the soothing sound of his deep melodic voice as he stroked my hair and kissed my face.

Kenyatta was the only man I'd ever felt safe with. He was the only man who'd ever bought me nice things and taken me to nice places, the only man who'd ever told me I was beautiful, and showed me the difference between making love and fucking. I imagined him saying I love you again as we made love, love without pain. I imagined what it would be like to be his bride. On those nights, the heat and the darkness and the hard claustrophobic confines of my box, even the weight of the iron chains around my neck ankles and wrists, became more tolerable. Everything was tolerable if it meant he would love me.

I finished my food and Kenyatta removed my plate and walked me upstairs. I almost fell as I struggled with the weight of the chains. I had gone with him to purchase them. We'd bought them on a trip to San

Francisco from a fetish store on Folsom Street that had a custom welder on staff. Kenyatta had shown them pictures of iron shackles recovered from the Henrietta Marie, the oldest slave ship ever discovered. By the end of the weekend the shackles were complete. We laughed about what the baggage handlers at the airport would think when our luggage went through the X-ray machine. I laughed now despite myself. Kenyatta looked back at me with concern on his face, checking to make certain I hadn't gone insane. That made me laugh harder.

He brought me into the kitchen. I was on my knees crawling by this point from the weight of the iron chains. That was how Kenyatta preferred me anyway. He kicked a bucket and a brush over to me and ordered me to scrub the floor while he stood over me with his flail. I went to work dutifully. I was grateful just to be in the sunlight. I knew Kenyatta would be raping me soon. Watching me scrub the floor naked on my hands and knees always turned him on, plus I knew he'd have to be going to work soon and this would be his last opportunity. My neck muscles throbbed beneath the weight of my shackles. I couldn't have lifted my head no matter how much I wanted to. I wanted to see my beautiful master's face. I finished scrubbing the kitchen floor and Kenyatta brought the flail down across my backside ordering me into the hallway to scrub the porcelain tile. I had barely begun scrubbing when I felt Kenyatta's breath on the back of my neck, his chest against my back, the top of his thighs against the backs of mine. I let out a sigh as the weight of his body crushed down on top of me.

CHAPTER II

I was molested by a cousin as a child. I don't say that to explain why I'm with Kenyatta. I don't hate all white men for the degeneracy of one. I say it to explain all the fucked up choices I made before meeting him. It's true that I hate my father. Not because he was a drunken asshole who beat my mother (though he was), but because all he did to my cousin was kick his ass. That solved everything in his mind. No police were called. I never went to counseling. My parents never even spoke to me about it. They never told me that what happened wasn't my fault. They swept it under the rug, turned it into a dirty secret, and advised me to do the same. I never could. I still wake up screaming with his taste in my mouth. My parents never told me that what happened didn't make me a bad person. So it did.

I started sleeping around, got pregnant, lost the baby, started doing drugs, got kicked out of the house, started using more drugs, moved to Las Vegas, got a job and started attending UNLV, met a lot of men and slept with most of them, got off drugs, began drinking more. Somehow, through all the drinking and partying, I managed to squeak my way through college. I got a B.A.

in English with a guaranteed student loan that has been in default for five or six years, got my teaching credentials and started teaching English at a middle school in Green Valley. I continued drinking and partying and sleeping with the wrong men, barely managing to drag my tired ass out of bed each morning to teach spelling and grammar and literature to kids who didn't want to hear anything poetic unless it was accompanied by a drumbeat and included the words "bitch" and "ho" interspersed at regular intervals. Then I met Kenyatta. None of the rest of that shit matters. This is where the story begins.

From the moment I met him I didn't think I was good enough for him, which is weird considering that I come from a family that thinks the polite word for African Americans is "coloreds," and they don't use the polite word much. Kenyatta was so different from everyone else I'd ever met. There was something so regal about him, something princely. His eyes were wise and strong, cruel at times, but even that was sexy. His voice was deep, Lou Rawls/Barry White type basso profundo. Sultry, smooth, and sensuous, yet still forceful and commanding. I hate telling you that he was surprisingly articulate. I know that sounds like some kind of off-handed racial insult. As if I'm implying that most black men are not. The ones I'd fucked in the past definitely weren't, neither were the rednecks, junkies, and trailer trash. I didn't come from a world of articulate people. It had taken four years of college to correct my own trailer park drawl. So that was the first thing that impressed me about him. His voice, his words, his eyes.

Those were the things that made me think I could love him. His body was what made me want to fuck him.

We'd met at a nightclub six years before when he was still married. I was walking upstairs to the bar and he was walking downstairs. He was wearing this tight black nylon shirt that hugged his chest and biceps in a way that would have made most men look effeminate but looked sexy as hell on him. Muscles seemed to be bulging from everywhere. My girlfriend and I looked up at him, smiling from ear to ear because he was fucking huge and gorgeous and he was looking at us. We passed on the stairs and his eyes bored into mine. He wasn't smiling, just staring, staring in a way that made his intentions absolutely clear. There was such raw sexuality in that stare that it made the temperature in the room jump and the moisture on my body increase, especially between my thighs. I felt like I should have said something, but no words would come, so I just stared back, smiling nervously and perspiring.

He turned to look back up at us as he continued down the stairs and we turned and looked down at him. His eyes went from my friend Tina back to me and then to Tina again. I knew the look. He was deciding which one of us to pursue. I would have laid bets that he wouldn't have picked me, not with Tina standing there.

My girlfriend Tina was thin and pretty and easy and drunk. She had fake breasts that still barely increased her bra-size to a C-cup. She was dressed in a tight baby-t to show off the surgeon's work and her thin waist. The mini-skirt she wore just barely covered her tight little ass and her legs were long and slender. She dressed like a slut because that's exactly what she was and she wanted to make sure that every man in the club knew it. I was sure she would wind up sucking his dick in the parking lot if he wanted her to. When he started walking back up the stairs toward us, I was certain the evening would end with her head bobbing up and down in his lap while I waited for her at the bar. When he walked right past her and took my hand I almost fainted. I was fat then, not obese, not the kind of fat that made people pity me. I was just a little chubby, thighs thicker than I would have liked, hips wider, ass bigger. My waist was actually rather small for a large woman though I still had that unsightly bulge where my lower abs should have been. Tina had once called it my FUPA—Fat Upper Pussy Area. I hated her for that even though I laughed when she said it. Laughing is what fat girls are taught to do when insulted. It is the most common defense mechanism in the world. That's why I was so surprised by Kenyatta's actions. I knew I was fat and men didn't often pass up women who looked like my friend Tina for women who looked like me.

"Hello, ladies. My name is Kenyatta."

His voice was deep and warm, and he continued to hold my hand and look into my eyes when he spoke to me, still ignoring my Barbie-like friend, still looking at me like I was something on a dessert tray.

"M-my name is Natasha and this is my friend Tina."

He never looked at her. Not even once. He kept his eyes on me the entire time.

"Are you ladies having a good time this evening?"

"We're doing great," Tina interjected.

Kenyatta turned toward her, looked her up and down, then turned back to me. I didn't even have to look at Tina to know she was insulted. I looked at him quizzically, wondering what his game was. Then I turned to Tina and shrugged my shoulders. I didn't know what I could have possibly done to single myself out for his attention, what might have made me stand out above Tina. Tina looked pissed. She crossed her arms beneath her hard surgically enhanced breasts, pushing them up even further so that there would be no mistaking what she had to offer, and started tapping her foot impatiently waiting for him to notice her. Kenyatta seemed to enjoy ignoring her. I began to wonder if he was just using me to get a rise out of her.

He began asking me about myself, where I was from, what I did for a living, what I did for fun, why I was at the club tonight. He never let go of my hand and never broke eye contact.

"I'm a teacher. I teach seventh and eighth grade English."

"Cool. You like kids?"

"Most of the time. Sometimes it can be rough. I used to work at a group home for girls when I was in college. The whole reason I went to school was so that I could get a job helping children. I thought I wanted to be a social worker or a child psychiatrist for a while."

"That's really cool that you were that into helping kids."

"Yeah, but after a year of working at the group home I quit and switched my major to English. I was having nightmares every night. I just couldn't detach myself from those kids. I'm too sensitive for that kind of work. I was depressed all the time. You'd be amazed what some of these girls had gone through, violence, abuse, rape, I just couldn't take it. Half the black girls that walked in there were crack babies and half the white ones had Fetal Alcohol Syndrome or mothers that were on meth. They didn't have a chance in hell. Sometimes I felt like someone should just drop a bomb on the entire ghetto."

"Fuck did you say?"

Kenyatta's face twisted up into a snarl as he spat his words out at me in anger. I pulled back, fearing for a second that he was about to physically attack me. He sensed my anxiety and did his best to relax his features and his posture. When he spoke again it was in calm measured tones.

"*I'm* from one of those ghettos and not everyone in there is smoking crack."

"Yeah, but you're an exception. The majority of them are."

Again, I could see that it was taking everything he had not to lose his temper.

"No. The majority of them are not. The majority of the people in the ghetto are hardworking honest folks who were just given less opportunity than most. When you live in an environment where violence, drugs, and gangs are everywhere, coupled with the worst educational system imaginable, it takes an exceptional individual to crawl up out of that mess. I wasn't an exceptional individual. I just had an exceptional mom who made sure that I never went to any of the neighborhood schools. She faked our address and gave me bus fare so that I could go to schools in predominantly white areas where the quality of education was better. If she hadn't done that I'd probably be stuck right there in the ghetto with the rest of the kids I grew up with."

"You can't blame all the ills of the ghetto on education."

"You're a teacher and you don't believe that education has that great an impact? Do you know that every single kid I know who went to my neighborhood high school instead of a magnet school or a Catholic high school or something is still right back there in the ghetto and most of them have drug habits or criminal records or both? They can trace seventy-five percent of the prison population in Oakland back to three high schools. Eighty percent of the prison population in America never graduated from high school. Rather than blowing the ghetto up or putting it under martial law they need to spend all that money they're currently spending on more police and bigger prisons and put it into building better schools with better teachers. I mean, no offense, but when I was growing up teachers weren't kids fresh out of college. The teachers I had were the same ones who taught my parents. Back then teaching was a career not a job. Not something you did for a while until something better came along. I mean, if you don't believe that education makes a difference why are you even doing it?"

"Because I love kids. But you wouldn't know what it's like trying to teach children nowadays. I don't exactly work in some rough inner-city school, but I do get a fair mixture of kids and you can almost tell the income level of each child by how well they perform in school. I couldn't imagine what it would be like if I had to walk through a metal detector every morning and have security walk me to my car every afternoon after work. How the hell do you teach kids like that?"

Kenyatta's nostrils flared.

"I can understand it might be easier for a kid to concentrate who has a full stomach when he comes to school, who didn't wake up in the middle of the night to the sound of gunfire and have to hide in the bathtub because stray bullets were coming through the walls, who wasn't listening to police helicopters thundering overhead all night long, who wasn't dodging gang members, drug pushers, crack heads and crack whores everyday walking to and from school. Poor kids have a lot going against them, but that doesn't make them any less intelligent or any more inherently violent. It just means that teachers have to work a little harder to keep them on track."

"I do work hard. I give those kids everything I've got every day!"

"How can you when every time you see some poor black kid walk into your room you've already labeled him in your mind as a lost cause?"

"It has nothing to do with black or white. We've got white kids from the trailer parks who are in the same boat."

"Yeah, but do you treat them the same? You don't because you can relate to the kids from the trailer park.

You clean up well, but I can still hear the faint hint of white trash country twang in your voice. It must have been hard work getting rid of that accent. I know. I had to do it too. My ghetto slur. Gangsta drawl. So, you can understand the white trailer trash, but not the black ghetto rats, am I right? Don't answer now. Right now you'll just get defensive. You won't answer honestly. You're going to tell me what you think or hope is true, not what you know is true. Go back to work tomorrow and just test yourself. Watch how you interact with each kid and tell me if you're giving them all the same level of attention. I think you'll be surprised."

I stuck out my chin and rolled my eyes in self-righteous indignation. Who was this guy to talk to me like he knew me? He didn't know shit about me. How dare he call me a damn racist? I jabbed a finger at his chest.

"I'll do that. That's fine. But let me ask you something, how much good do you think people like you are doing those kids by being apologists for them? By making excuses for them and blaming their environment or the educational system or institutionalized racism or the government or slavery or whatever? How much good do you think you're doing them with all of that?"

He smirked and shook his head.

"A hell of a lot more than those who ignore them. Look, you've got a difficult job. No question. And I applaud you and all teachers for what you do. Putting up with these hardheaded kids can't be easy. But if every school had enough qualified teachers, if they had enough books, enough computers, enough classrooms, smaller class sizes, so that they could actually do their jobs, if we flipped the script and started spending as much or more on giving a kid an education as we do on locking their asses up once they slip between the cracks, don't you think your job would be easier?"

"Yes, yes it would. And you're right. And I probably sound to you like some out of touch racist asshole."

"Not at all. Out of touch? Perhaps. Racist. No. If you're not from there how would you know what it's like?"

"Well, you were right. I grew up in a trailer. I was as poor as any kid in the ghetto so I know a little bit about poverty."

"Yeah, but crime is very different in a trailer park than it is in a crowded inner-city neighborhood."

"Different but not better or worse. You don't see many kids leaving the trailer park for Ivy League schools either."

"I'm sure."

"Look, I'm sorry. I know I've probably turned you completely off…"

"I'm not trippin'. I don't expect white people to have a clue about the black experience. All your opinions are media created and the American media has an interest in demonizing the black male. Monsters sell newspapers and the young black male has become the American monster."

"Yeah, and black people also have an interest in demonizing the white male and the white female for that matter. We make great scapegoats."

I couldn't help but smile when I said it. It was hard to believe I was in the middle of a crowded dance club with the most beautiful black man I'd ever seen having a political debate about race. It was just too surreal.

"You're just baiting me now. Look, I have no animosity at all toward white women. You may not realize it, but white men have oppressed you as much as they have our people. Woman is the nigger of the world."

"You're quoting John Lennon?"

"Actually, I think that was Yoko Ono. I could quote Malcolm X if you'd prefer?"

"Now who's baiting who?"

"You started it."

He smiled again, and again my heart did that little flutter. I couldn't remember a man ever affecting me this way. It was disconcerting as hell.

"Sure, okay, women have it hard. Black people have it hard. So what are we supposed to do? Cry in our beer and blame everybody else while our lives continue to turn to shit?"

"Nope. We succeed and prosper despite of. Success is the best revenge."

He winked at me when he said it as if we were some sort of co-conspirators. I smiled again and then laughed.

"Okay, I like that."

"Still, once we get ours we have to go back to help those who may not have met with the same success.

Like I said, I escaped the 'hood because I didn't go to the neighborhood school and so I got a decent education. I was lucky, pure and simple. But that school graduates six-hundred students a year. *Six hundred!* Those who don't end up in prison or on drugs end up on welfare or in minimum wage jobs, which is to say, right back in the ghetto. And there are hundreds of schools just like it all across the country. We can't just turn our backs on them or flush the entire ghetto down the toilet. They deserve a piece of the American dream as much as the next man. We've got to help because the frustrated and ignored student of today is the drug-dealing, drug addicted murderer of tomorrow. Believe that."

I nodded in agreement. Damn, I liked this man.

"You should be a politician."

"A black politician who hangs out at nightclubs pickin' up white girls wouldn't really go over too well."

"That's probably true. You would have to give up the white girls."

"Would you miss me?"

His smile looked almost predatory now as he leaned in closer to me and reached out to stroke my cheek with the back of his hand.

"We ain't quite that tight yet."

"We will be," he said as he leaned in closer and brushed my hair away from my ear.

"Oh really?" I tried to sound cocky, but my knees were shaking.

His lecherous grin widened again into that big confident smile. His eyes softened then he shook his head and chuckled. He gave my hand a slight squeeze and pulled me closer until our bodies touched.

"You are beautiful," he whispered in my ear.

"A beautiful, ignorant racist?" I blushed, thinking of some of the things I'd said earlier. I don't know what the hell I'd been thinking. If ever there was a time for political correctness it was when talking to a six-six, two-hundred and sixty pound black man, especially when you were attracted to him.

"No. Just beautiful."

How Kenyatta could have not been offended by some of the things I'd said was beyond belief. I kept wondering if he just wanted to fuck me so bad that he was suppressing the urge to pimp-slap me every time I said something stupid. But if all he wanted was some ass then why wasn't he hittin' on Tina? It's not like it was difficult to tell that the girl was easy.

He stood there staring at me without saying a word as I looked at him and then looked away and blushed then looked back again only to find him still staring at me, causing me to turn away and blush again. It was the most sexually charged moment I'd ever had inside a nightclub and I've had sex in nightclubs before. But this was somehow more intense than any of the drunken groping and thrusting I'd done previously. All he was doing was holding my hand and staring at my face, but it was like I could feel him all over me. I forgot all about Tina. I forgot I was in a nightclub and forgot that Kenyatta was some stranger I'd just met. I felt like I was falling in love. But I didn't believe in love at first sight.

"I have to go soon. Why don't you give me your number and I'll call you."

"Why are you so interested in me? I know I just pissed you off with that little conversation and my friend would probably fuck you right now."

He pulled back and looked at me. The smile was gone, but his eyes still had that warm consoling look in them along with that playful hint of mischief.

"Who says I want to fuck her? She's drunk and conceited and you're beautiful and sweet and yes, a little naive when it comes to race, but who isn't?"

"I was getting you pissed off though wasn't I?"

"Yeah, well, I tend to get a little worked up when it comes to racial issues. What black man in this country doesn't?"

"So, then why even bother fucking with white girls? Why not just stick to black women? I'm sure they'd understand you better."

"There's a hell of a lot more to me than just the color of my skin. Just because a woman's black doesn't necessarily mean she'll understand me any more than you do. Sure, she'll get the race thing. But there's much more to me than that. Besides, that would be playing it safe now wouldn't it? What fun would it be if we all just stayed in our comfort zones? I believe in expanding my horizons. Besides, I'm taking Dick Gregory's advice and trying to wipe out the white race by having sex with all the white women I can. I'm gonna breed you right out of existence."

I laughed.

"You are crazy."

"It could work though. That's one crusade I could start without looking like a hypocrite. I could convince every black man in the country to sleep with white women and create a master race of mixed babies."

"There is something seriously wrong with you."

I was laughing so hard that tears were coming out of my eyes.

"You're right. The sistas would definitely hate me. That would leave them with nothin' but white boys. I'd wind up gettin' my ass assassinated. So what do you think?" Do you think I should stick to my own kind? You're not into brothers?"

I looked down at the floor, shuffling my feet nervously. Kenyatta reached out and lifted my chin so I was looking into his intense eyes again.

"I'm into you," I answered, shrugging. "I'm into whatever feels right."

"And do I feel right?"

I looked at his massive shoulders and bulging chest, his thick biceps and that flawless smile filled with perfectly straight, perfectly white teeth, the high cheekbones, and smoldering black eyes. He was intelligent and he had a sense of humor. I didn't care what color he was. He was damn-near perfect.

"Yeah, you do."

"Then give me your number so I can call you sometime."

He pulled me close to him again, wrapping his arms around my waist and hugging me, still staring into my eyes.

"You are weird. I can't really figure out what your deal is. But okay, I'll give you my number."

I wrote my phone number down and he took it and placed it in his pocket. Then he took my hand again and pulled me close to him once more.

"Give me a hug before I leave."

I smiled and almost laughed.

"Are you serious?"

"You don't want to hug me?"

I wrapped my arms around him and he leaned down and kissed my neck and shoulders then breathed heavy in my ear as he spoke in that deep luxurious voice of his.

"I'll call you."

"Yeah, sure you will."

He did. He called me from work two days later while I was sitting at home in my t-shirt with what looked like a sea of bills spread out in front of me, wondering how I was going to pay off the two payday loans I'd taken out weeks before without taking out another one. When the phone rang I almost leaped for it, eager to have something to take my mind off my finances even if it was just Tina calling to brag about her latest sexual conquest or cry about her latest heartbreak.

"Natasha?"

"Yes? Who's calling?" I was smiling already. I recognized the voice.

"This is Kenyatta."

My heart did a somersault. I knew Tina had been betting he wouldn't call. She was still certain he'd just been fucking with her and that the next time she went to the club he'd be there trying to get into her well-traveled panties. I couldn't wait to tell her she was wrong.

"Oh, hi. I didn't think you'd call."

There was a long pause.

"Where do you live?"

"Excuse me?"

"I want to come visit you. Where do you live?"

"I don't even know you." I almost giggled when I spoke, like some shy schoolgirl. Something about his voice was making me crazy.

"Well, you're not going to get to know me over the phone. I hate talking on the phone."

"I'm not into booty calls."

"Then let's not make this one."

I didn't even know what the hell he meant by that. He could have said anything to me and it would have worked. I didn't care if it was a one night stand or not. I just wanted to look at him again. I wanted to see him look at me again, the way he had at the club, like I was the most desirable woman on earth. I should have been immune to all of this. I'd heard every line by men who just wanted to get inside me and then get out with as little hassle as possible. Men who called you their dream girl one day and then didn't call you at all after you'd let them in your bed. But no matter how many times I'd been fucked over by men there was always a part of me that hoped the next one would be different. So I gave him the directions to my house.

I almost laughed when he showed up at my door wearing a suit and tie. I had never asked him what he did for a living, but whatever I had assumed certainly didn't involve a business suit.

"Hi! Come on in."

He walked into my apartment, removed his suit jacket, looked around, dropped the suit jacket onto the back of one of my kitchen chairs then casually reclined on my couch. If you didn't know any better you'd have sworn he had been there a thousand times.

"Come sit with me."

He held out his hand and I took it. His palms were rough and calloused, but the back of his hands were smooth as a woman's. Even that I found strangely exciting. He continued holding my hand as I walked around from the back of the couch to the front and took a seat beside him. I was nervous as hell. He seemed so casual. Not the nervous excitement guys normally have when they enter a woman's apartment for the first time and the possibility of sex is there. He was either confident that I would fuck him or he didn't care either way. I was starting to perspire again.

I sat next to him and he hugged me and kissed me on my neck again.

"I wanted to hang out with you and get to know you a little. Just don't get offended if I fall asleep. It's not a comment on your company. I worked sixteen hours straight yesterday and then spent two hours in the gym this morning before going back to work today. I'm exhausted."

"What do you do?"

"I make money, lots of it. I'm not wealthy, but I'm comfortable."

"Don't be mysterious. Whenever a guy in this town gets all mysterious about his occupation it usually means he's either a drug dealer or a pimp."

"I'm no pimp."

"Drug dealer?"

"That would fit the stereotype wouldn't it? But no, sorry to disappoint you. I'm a real estate broker and I'm also part owner of a boxing gym."

"I didn't mean just because you were black. There are white drug dealers too. My brother was arrested for running a meth lab. He was mysterious about his occupation too."

"Okay, well now there's no more mystery."

Every time I opened my mouth in his presence I seemed to step on some racial landmine. I had to do something to turn the conversation back around.

"You box?"

"A little. Nothing serious. I'm not pro or anything. I'm more interested in the business side of things. I'm part owner of a little gym on Sahara and Rainbow. It's not like a real boxer's gym. It's for guys like me who want to learn to box but don't actually want to fight. Mostly executives who want to let out a little aggression and feel like tough guys and housewives trying to lose weight. I make a lot of contacts there for my real estate business. Anyone who buys a house from me gets one month free membership to my gym. We get a lot of law enforcement guys in there too, cops, military, even Feds. I never get speeding tickets because of that place."

Sometimes it was all about asking the right questions.

"So you're like an entrepreneur? That's cool. I'd have never guessed. I mean I figured you were some kind of athlete by the way you look, maybe a basketball or football player. I just never figured you for owning your own business and selling houses."

"You just figured I was some dumb jock, right? Either a pimp a drug pusher or a basketball player. You are just full of prejudgments aren't you?"

Another landmine successfully detonated.

"I'm not gonna lie. You don't usually meet guys like you walking around night clubs."

"Then why go?"

I shrugged.

"Where else are you going to go? Why were you there? How the hell do you find time with everything that you do?"

"I hate sleeping alone."

"You don't have a girlfriend?"

"Not right now, I don't."

"Why not?"

"I'm too busy and my life is complicated enough. That's what I've been telling myself anyway, but now I think having a girlfriend might help uncomplicate my life a little. It would at least keep me out of the nightclubs."

The guy said all the right things. Rich, intelligent, well-built, looking for commitment. Something had to be wrong with him.

"So, if you hate sleeping alone then why didn't you try to get me to come home with you on Saturday?"

"I also hate making mistakes. You aren't one night stand material. You're the type of woman men fall in love with. Now, your little blonde friend, *she* was one night stand material. I made a choice and decided I was more up for falling in love than getting head in the parking lot."

"You saw all of that just by looking at me?"

"I saw most of it. Talking to you confirmed it."

"Why? Because I like to argue?"

"Because you've got more on your mind than last night's episode of *Desperate Housewives* or what the latest designer drug is and because you've got guts but you're also really sensitive, really sweet, and really lonely. I could see your loneliness like a beacon in that nightclub. Some men could take advantage of that. I'm not that type of man. I've been that type of man, but I'm not anymore. I knew I had more of a potential to get sprung on a woman like you than to use her and discard her."

"I don't even know what to say to that. It almost sounds like you're proposing."

"I'm proposing we get to know each other better and letting you know that I'm serious."

I hesitated. This was just too fucking weird.

"First you call me up sounding like you just want to get some and now you come over and tell me that you might, if the stars are right and the moon is in Pluto, be able to fall in love with me even though you don't even know me? But all you really want to do is just fall asleep on my couch?"

He laughed.

"Yeah, that's about right. I mean, I'd prefer to make love to you. I just don't want to rush things. Okay, I do want to rush things. I'm just fucking tired."

I laughed too then.

"I wouldn't have let you anyway. I'm not that kind of girl...not anymore anyway. I've been celibate for almost a year and I'm enjoying my life without men...less bullshit to deal with. I've gotten burned way too often. I'm taking it slow from now on."

Kenyatta smiled and something in his eyes glittered. I recognized the look. He was warming to the challenge. I was both excited and disappointed by it. It was such a typical male response. But I wanted him too.

He reached out and stroked my hair, pushing it out of my face and back behind my ears. Then he kissed me. It was a slow passionate kiss. His lips pecked at mine, once, twice, before he sealed them to my mouth and sucked my breath away.

We kissed and stroked each other for more than an hour. He delicately caressed my neck, back, and arms with his fingertips. Raising goose bumps wherever he touched me and sending tingles and chills all over my flesh. He raised my shirt and rubbed his face against my breasts and stomach, nuzzling like a kitten. I lost all control of myself. I didn't care about being a good girl and not having sex on the first date. I didn't care anymore if he thought I was a slut. I just wanted him. He sucked my nipples into his mouth, and I moaned unselfconsciously as he flicked his tongue across them, gently biting until I screamed for him to make love to me.

As soon as the words left my mouth Kenyatta withdrew his lips from my breasts and sat back onto the couch, smiling with satisfaction. I realized then that I had fucked up. It wasn't about the sex for him, but about the control. Now that I'd gone back on everything I'd just said to him about taking it slow there was no need for him to actually fuck me. He had his victory, his conquest. It wouldn't have surprised me if he had gotten up and left.

"Why don't you tell me more about yourself instead?"

My pelvis was making small circles and I was actually whimpering. I wanted him so badly. I couldn't believe he wasn't going to fuck me.

"But...but don't you want to..."

"We should probably take it slow like you said. Plus, I am still tired."

I wanted to kill him. Instead, I started another argument.

"You were right."

"Right about what?"

"About me treating poor white kids differently than I treat poor black kids. When I was in my class today, I paid attention to the way I interacted with each of the children and I definitely have a bias. It's wrong, but it's there. I really don't think it's avoidable. Everyone has their prejudices."

"Yeah, but some are more destructive than others. Those kids might look at you and think you're some spoiled white woman who grew up with her daddy giving her everything she wanted and that could be the farthest thing from the truth, but it doesn't really hurt you for them to think that because they have no power over you. You're in a position of authority over them so your prejudice is more destructive."

"I'm agreeing with you that it's wrong for me to think this way, but it's just as wrong if some kid in my class looks at me and assumes that I'm some over-privileged spoiled brat. There are no degrees of prejudice."

"There is justifiable prejudice though."

"What? Now *you* sound like the racist here."

"I'm saying that because of the way black people have been oppressed in this society it is understandable if they feel a certain hostility toward your race."

"That is absolute bullshit. You're trying to tell me that because I'm white it's wrong for me to hold negative feelings toward black people, but it's okay for black people to hate me for my color?"

"Not okay, but understandable."

"So are you trying to say that black people can't be racists?"

"Of course not. That would be absurd. All I'm trying to say is that it's easier to understand the hate that hate made. It's easy to understand why the underprivileged kid who has nothing resents the privileged child who has everything and has acquired it at his expense. What's hard to understand is how the privileged child can hate the underprivileged kid. That's just plain evil."

"Shit, I'm not privileged! I had to work hard for everything I've gotten in life. I've been stepped on and beaten down as much as anybody."

"That's just a metaphor. When I say privileged, I'm talking about the rights that everyone should have but that minorities in the country do not. The right to not be denied jobs, promotions, equal pay, fair treatment under law, equal representation in government, the right to walk into a store and not be followed every second by security, to drive a nice car without getting stopped and harassed by the police, to stand before a judge and not receive a harsher sentence than members of the racial majority, all because of the color of your skin. When it comes to those basic rights white people are the privileged majority."

"So that makes it okay for you to hate us?"

"Not okay, understandable. White people are in a position of power that we are not. Just like with the kids that you teach, your racism can cause them far more harm than theirs can cause you. You grade their assignments, you determine what their assignments will be, you decide which students you will put the most effort into and which ones you won't. Likewise, the ruling majority, the white people in this country determine how many tax dollars will be spent on improving education and providing opportunity for minorities. The predominantly Caucasian corporate leaders determine how high they will allow a minority employee to climb. The predominantly white juries across America and the predominantly white judges and lawmakers determine what kind of treatment a minority will get when he enters a courtroom. Your prejudice has the ability to cause us much greater harm than we could ever cause you."

"All prejudice is still wrong."

"No argument there. I'm not condoning anyone's prejudice. I wish that everyone could be judged on their own individual merits alone without bearing the weight of their entire race. It's not fair to anyone. But when that shit is coming from a white person, it's a hundred times more destructive."

I could tell Kenyatta was still steaming when he left my apartment. He didn't even hug or kiss me, just smiled, waved, and walked out the door. I wouldn't have been at all surprised if I'd never seen him again. When he came back the next day I was determined not to start another argument with him. I needn't have worried.

Kenyatta walked in, grabbed me in his arms and kissed me hard while brutishly ripping my nightgown in half. I didn't care that I'd paid almost fifty dollars for that gown at Victoria's Secret and would probably never replace it. I just wanted this man. The front door was still open when he laid me on the floor and fucked me like some whore he'd plucked off the corner, hard and aggressive. Just like I liked it. He bit my face and neck so hard he left bruises. My ass was likewise tattooed with his hand print in livid red and purple. At one point he'd even used his belt on me, leaving welts on my back and buttocks as I knelt on my hands and knees and he fucked me hard from behind. I screamed when I came. Then I begged him for more.

"Oh my God! That was incredible! Don't stop. Fuck me again, Daddy!"

Abruptly, without the slightest warning, Kenyatta pulled me onto his lap, belly across his knees, forehead brushing the floor, ass in the air. He never asked me if I was into being dominated or spanked. He just did it. Before I could say a word, his palm came down on my ass.

"What the—"

He spanked me again and again, reddening my ass cheeks and raising welts. Then he bit me. He leaned down and seized my still sore and throbbing buttocks in his mouth and bit down hard.

"Ahhhhhh! Fuuuuuck! Stop!"

I couldn't believe he'd just bitten me. It was somehow more disturbing than the spanking. Yet, I was powerfully aroused by it all. He rolled me off his lap and stood. I was still lying there on the living room floor with my legs quivering and my breaths coming in short rapid bursts, Kenyatta's sweat and semen drying on my belly, when he stooped, picked up his clothes, and began to dress himself.

"You're leaving?"

"I'll be back."

"When?"

"Tomorrow."

"So what was this? Why'd you bite me? What was that spanking for," I asked still trying to catch my breath.

"Fun. I'll be back."

He turned and walked out the door leaving a noticeable absence as if he'd taken a part of me with him. After being single for years, I suddenly felt incredibly alone. If Kenyatta never came back, I knew I'd miss him forever. I couldn't remember ever feeling that way about anyone. I reached down and rubbed my ass where Kenyatta had spanked me. It was still warm, raw, and sore, sensitive to the touch. When I pulled my hands away, my fingertips were red. He had drawn blood. I stood and locked the front door behind him then ran to the bathroom. Kenyatta may have gone, but he had left me with something, his signature. His teeth marks were embedded in my left buttock. He had broken the skin and the indent of each tooth was clearly visible. Blood dribbled down the back of my leg. I smiled, remembering the feel of the mouth that had caused the damage. I dreamed about him all evening, rubbing my wounded ass and wondering if there was something wrong with me that I had enjoyed the pain, enjoyed submitting to this man I barely knew.

Chapter III

He swatted my mop bucket away and it skidded across the floor, splashing suds and water onto the tile. I squeezed the wet rag in my hand as he smacked my bare ass. I knew what was next.

I moaned in ecstasy as much as pain, anticipating his length filling me. I felt his rough hands grab my hips, his strong fingers kneading the flesh, gripping hard as he forced his solid length inside of me. He entered easily. I was already wet from anticipation. Still, my breath caught in my throat as his flesh entered mine. His cock was so long it still caused me pain even after all these months. That first thrust felt as if the head of his cock jabbed my ribcage. I gasped in shock then moaned again as a shudder went from between my thighs all the way up my spine. He felt so good I wanted to scream. I could feel his hard chest against my back, his thighs against the back of mine, his breath against my cheek, as he thrust that magnificent organ of his deeper inside of me.

"I love you, master. I love you," I said.

His only reply was a tug of my hair and his teeth sinking into my shoulder as he pounded deeper within me. I collapsed to the tile floor, unable to support myself on my hands and knees with both his weight and the weight of the chains pressing down on me. He continued to fuck me, harder now. He pulled my hips hard against him to meet his thrusts. Our rhythm was now something violent and powerful. He smacked my ass over and over as he fucked me. I felt his thumb lubed with saliva slide between my buttocks and into my ass and I knew what was coming next. He was so large that I had always had difficulty taking him this way. So, of course he had made anal sex a regular part of our love-play. Now he was even less gentle than normal. He went slow at first, easing it in inch by inch as he held himself up on his powerful arms and gradually descended until his entire length slid inside me. It was excruciating. I felt my stomach cramp as his erection pulsed and pounded within my distended rectum. Then he became more forceful, aggressively jack-hammering his thick cock in and out of my ass as if he were trying to drive me right through the floorboards. He reached around and wrapped one of his massive biceps around my throat and constricted until my windpipe slammed shut.

Between the pain in my anus and the sudden loss of oxygen, I began to panic. Spots danced before my eyes and I thrashed and bucked, panicking as everything began to go dark, trying to free myself. I scratched at his hands and arms and tried to pry his arm from around my throat, but it was like trying to bend iron. Then he reached his other arm beneath me as he dropped his entire weight onto my back, still thrusting relentlessly.

His fingers found my clitoris easily and he slipped his index finger first inside me to wet it with my juices before flicking it rapidly back and forth across my swollen clit. The pain, the loss of oxygen, and now the delirious sensations radiating from my sex brought me to the most explosive orgasm I could remember. Every muscle contracted as if shocked with a taser and then vibrated and convulsed as waves of ecstasy tore through my helpless body. My arms and legs thrashed and kicked. My back arched and a scream tore from my throat as Kenyatta finally relaxed his grip. My asshole contracted around my master's cock and I came again while Kenyatta continued fucking my sore and swollen anus with his mesomorphic organ, still fingering my engorged clit. He bit the back of my neck and growled and I knew he was about to cum. He withdrew his cock from my asshole abruptly. It felt as if he had turned it inside out. I screamed in pain and my guts cramped again. My rectum was so badly chafed it felt like it was on fire. Kenyatta grabbed one of my arms and turned me over.

"Look at me!"

He had his cock in his hand, squeezing it tight, as he knelt above me, straddling my chest with that magnificent organ dangling inches from my lips. Finally, I was able to look up at his face. He was so gorgeous. I smiled as his seed rained down upon my face. I licked it from my lips, relishing the salty taste of his semen as it dribbled down my cheeks and onto my lips.

"You look beautiful like that," Kenyatta said smiling. He used one finger to scoop some of his semen off my chin and spoon it into my mouth. I sucked it from his finger tip, twirling my tongue along the tip of his finger the way I did when I sucked his cock. A shudder went through him.

"Stick out your tongue."

I did as I was told and Kenyatta squeezed out the last of his semen onto my outstretched tongue.

"This is my body. This is my blood," he said with a seriousness and solemnity that would have been comical from anyone but him.

He had once told me that swallowing his cum to him was like taking communion with a God. It made him feel powerful to watch me lick his seed from my lips. It made me feel so submissive that I always wanted to make love immediately afterward or to be hugged and cuddled in his powerful arms or to curl up at the feet of my master like a lap dog, which is usually what I settled for. This time he just handed me back my bucket and walked upstairs to dress for work.

"Have that floor clean by the time I'm ready to leave."

I was forbidden even to say, "Yes, Master" now. None of the abductees aboard the slave ships spoke English yet so neither was I allowed to. Instead I nodded my head and picked up my scrub brush. Feeling the absence of him as a hollow place in my heart and every orifice he'd entered.

Kenyatta came back down just as I finished the hallway. He looked amazing in his dark business suit and white shirt with gray pinstriped tie. He always dressed like he was running for president and it worked for him. He looked so handsome standing there like that

that my own sense of wretchedness increased. I knew what I must have looked like in comparison.

"Get below."

I crawled, dragging my chains. The iron collar around my neck cut deeper into my skin as the weight of the other chains attached to it dragged behind me. Blood from my neck dripped onto the tile floor I had just spent the last hour scrubbing insuring that there would be more work for me the next day. The humidity in the basement overwhelmed me after having been upstairs for even that brief period. It felt like I was walking through a wall of moist heat as I crossed the threshold. Kenyatta stood above me, watching, as I crawled. I knew that watching me crawl was one of the things that seemed to turn him on the most. He would have fucked me again, right there on the stairs if it wouldn't have gotten his suit dirty and made him late for work. The stairs scraped my knees as I crawled down them. I began to moan and then to cry as I dragged my broken body down into the basement and across the hard concrete floor.

"Back in your box now."

His voice was not angry or harsh but matter of fact as if he was merely giving direction to a child who needed to be reminded of such things, as if he was merely reminding me to brush my teeth or wash my hands before dinner. I crawled into the box and Kenyatta padlocked it and left without a word. He closed the basement door and both the heat and the darkness redoubled.

I was constantly thirsty, constantly hungry, miserable from sunrise to sunset except for those brief moments when Kenyatta brought me out to fuck me or whip me or both. His cock inside of me was the only joy in my life now. Perhaps that was the other lesson he was trying to teach me, that I needed him.

The lingering taste of Kenyatta's semen recalled the vivid memory of the first time I'd taken his manhood between my lips. Kenyatta was the first man I'd given a blowjob to since my first blowjob. I had hated the act. When I was raped as a child, the taste and texture of my abuser's semen, the stench of his unwashed testicles, had stuck with me for years. I would wake up screaming with that taste on my lips. The first time Kenyatta asked me to suck his cock, I had refused, repulsed by the very idea of it.

"I-I don't do that."

Kenyatta raised an eyebrow and stared at me curiously.

"A woman who doesn't give head is only half a woman. Show me a woman who doesn't suck her man's cock and I'll show you a man who is looking for any and every opportunity to cheat on her. I won't tell you, you'd do it if you loved me. Not because it isn't true, but because it's too cliché. I will say that if you want to remain the only woman in my life, you will learn to please me."

He leaned back in his chair with his eyebrow still cocked, a smug expression on his face, awaiting my reply.

"Even if a woman is the best lover you ever had? If she does everything else perfectly, just the way you like it, but just doesn't suck your dick, that isn't enough?"

Kenyatta smirked and shook his head, eyes still boring into my skull like he was trying to read my thoughts.

"A woman who doesn't give head could never be the best lover I ever had and she wouldn't be my lover for long."

Kenyatta wasn't a man given to threats. He said it as a simple matter of fact. If I didn't give him head he would get it from someone else. The thought of losing him to some cum-guzzling slut almost brought tears to my eyes.

"I-I don't know how."

"I'll show you."

Kenyatta was a patient teacher. He calmly stood and unbuckled his pants, unzipped them and let them fall to his ankles. He wore silk boxers, black, with little red and gold paisleys on them. He let them slip down to his ankles as well. He guided me gently to my knees with just the slightest pressure from his manicured fingertips on my shoulders until my nose was level with the head of his turgid organ. He grabbed my jaw with his strong hand and slipped his thumb into my mouth.

"Suck it."

I did as instructed, sucking on his thumb.

"Swirl your tongue around the tip."

I obeyed.

"Now tickle the underside with your tongue."

Again, I obeyed, looking up at him, desperate for his approval.

"Now, slide it down your throat."

I took his thumb as deep in my mouth as it would go.

"In and out."

I slid his thumb in and out of my mouth, my eyes alternating from looking up at him and staring at his erect penis, which was still bobbing in the air, inches from my face.

"I don't feel your tongue."

I swirled my tongue around the tip of his thumb again as I continued sliding it in and out of my mouth. I flicked my tongue along the underside of his thumb as he had instructed me to do earlier.

"Now take it out of your mouth and lick up and down both sides."

I obeyed once more.

"Now, repeat. Do everything I told you to do, exactly the way I told you to do it, but now, I want you to do it to my cock."

I felt a tremor of fear and a brief moment of revulsion, but then I obeyed. I eased his engorged flesh between my lips and began bobbing my head up and down, sliding his cock in and out of my mouth. I flicked it with my tongue then swirled my tongue around the head like I was licking a lollipop. I licked up and down the shaft, and finally eased it as far down my throat as I could without gagging.

This was so different from the memory of my assault. Kenyatta wasn't ramming his cock down my throat, choking me with it. I felt in control. I could feel his organ pulsate, nearing orgasm, and each time I would ease it out of my throat and lick it up and down.

"Stroke it with your hand and lick the tip. Just like that, like you're licking an ice cream cone. Suck the tip."

I sucked and licked and stroked until I could feel him about to cum.

"I'm going to cum and I want you to drink every drop. You understand?"

I nodded my ascent as I continued bobbing my head up and down on his tumescent manhood. I tried to hide my panic at the idea of him filling my mouth with his semen, of being compelled to swallow it. I felt myself beginning to hyperventilate. I had to get myself back under control. I was beginning to feel nauseated and feared I would vomit when Kenyatta's cum filled my throat. That would almost certainly end things between us, I feared.

I tried to distract myself with other thoughts. I thought about how wonderful Kenyatta was. I recalled how his lips felt on my nipples, how his tongue felt on my clitoris. It was only fair that I reciprocate. Kenyatta was nothing like the fat cousin who had raped me in my parent's basement. I wondered if perhaps his cum would taste differently, if I might even enjoy it. I took his cock deeper, pushing it past my tonsils, choking myself, but not caring, wanting to please my man, and when I felt Kenyatta's body tense, heard his low, growling, guttural moan, felt that thick, warm, salty, eruption splash across my tonsils, I did as Kenyatta asked. I swallowed it all. That's when I knew how much I loved him. It wasn't long after that Kenyatta brought up the subject of the box.

I had already committed myself to the experiment by then, even though my insides roiled at the thought of being locked inside a wooden coffin for who knew how long, so I couldn't back down. I needed to see it through. But Kenyatta wanted me to know exactly what I was getting into and why. He pulled out a book he'd found at the library when he was a boy. I was surprised by the profoundness of his emotion as he opened the book.

"*Roots* had just come out on television and I was so affected by it that I wanted to know more about the slave trade and what had happened to our people two hundred years ago when they came to America. I asked my Mom about it and she took me to the library to look it up for myself."

He paused. His strong regal face cracked and trembled, twisting into a scowl as whatever he was feeling inside broke through to the surface and tears welled up in his eyes. He looked up at the ceiling and inhaled deeply, fighting to control his emotion. I could tell this was a painful memory for him. The chords in his neck bulged as his body tensed, struggling for control. When he looked back down at me, his face was hard and stoic. He forced himself to look me in the eyes, but I knew it was taking a great effort for him to do so. I knew he wanted to hang his head or lower his brow into his hands, anything but look at me. But it just wasn't his way to show weakness in front of me and giving in to his emotions would have seemed weak to him. I suspect he also knew that it would hurt me more to see the pain on his face as he struggled to suppress it.

"This was the book I picked up. It's called *400 Years of Oppression*. It contains, among other things, detailed descriptions of life aboard a slave ship pieced together from various accounts and historical documents, most of it told by former slaves who traveled through the Middle Passage. It contains slave narratives all the way up to the emancipation proclamation. It follows the life of African Americans from the time they were kidnapped from their homes in Africa, to the civil rights movement, right up to today's struggles with drugs, crime, and poverty. I cried when I read it. I wept out loud and I couldn't stop crying even when my mother held me in her arms. I had no idea how bad it was. I had no idea how many Africans they stole from their homes and brought here. In that book, they estimated that about fifteen million slaves were brought here from Africa and at least another five million never made the trip due to disease, malnourishment, suicide, murder, and slave revolts. Then all the hell they went through for more than four hundred years in this country as they struggled to find freedom and equality. I had no idea. You could not imagine what my people endured aboard those ships."

Kenyatta opened the book and I prepared for the worst. But just as he had been unprepared when he'd picked up the book twenty-five years ago. I was completely overwhelmed by what I heard. I could never have imagined that human beings could have been capable of such cruelty to one another.

"Africans were treated like cattle during the crossing, wedged together below deck as tight as they could pack them in, chained together and stuffed in narrow, three feet high compartments too low for standing. Most of these compartments had no light or fresh air except for those immediately under the grated hatchways. The stifling heat was unbearable, and the humid air nearly unbreathable.

"In the latter 18th century, most slave ships were "tight packers," squeezing as many slaves as they could fit into their cargo holds, crowded together in spaces smaller than a grave, stacked on top of one another like spoons, breathing each other's sweat and body odor. Disease and suffocation below deck were common. Men were often chained in pairs, manacled together in twos and threes, shackled wrist to wrist or ankle to ankle. They were forced to lie on their backs with their heads between the legs of others. This meant they often had to lie in each other's sweat, feces, urine, and, in the case of dysentery, even blood, covered from head to toe in lice and other parasites, a number of them in different stages of suffocation; many of them foaming at the mouth and in their last agonies, dying of oxygen deprivation.

"The floor of the ship's hold resembled a slaughterhouse covered with blood and mucus. The confined air was rendered noxious by the sweat, urine, feces, blood and vomit evacuated from their bodies and being repeatedly breathed."

I didn't want to hear anymore. I wanted to clap my hands to my ears and scream.

What he was describing was too horrible to have been possible. There was no way human beings could have done things like that to each other. But, I knew Kenyatta wasn't embellishing. I knew everything he was saying was true and I doubted he'd be able to approximate any of the horrors he was describing or whether I'd be able to endure it if he could.

"Diseases such as smallpox and yellow fever spread like wildfire, and slaves that fell ill were often thrown overboard to prevent wholesale epidemics.

"Some captains would have their crew periodically clean the "tween decks" with hot vinegar. Most did not. Slavers used iron muzzles and whippings to control the slaves who greatly outnumbered them on the overcrowded ships. Women were raped and sexually abused by the officers and the crew, who were permitted to indulge their passions at will and were sometimes guilty of such cruelties as would turn the stomach of a seasoned prostitute. Often, after suffering violent sexual abuses, women would leap overboard and drown themselves.

"But the constant deficit of fresh air was by far the most torturous of all the horrors aboard these ships. To bring in fresh oxygen, most slave ships had five or six air-ports on each side about five inches in length and four in width. Some had what they called wind-sails. But whenever the sea was rough and the rain heavy, the crew would shut these and every other opening in the ship and the slaves' living space soon became intolerably hot and, what little oxygen there was, almost unbreathable.

"Slaves often fainted from the oppressive heat and the deprivation of oxygen and were carried above deck where many of them died and were tossed overboard. A healthy slave was sometimes dragged up onto the deck shackled to a corpse; sometimes of the three attached to the same chain, one was dying and another dead. Suffocating slaves struggled to extricate themselves, destroying one another in their fury and desperation for oxygen and room. Men strangled those next to them, and women clawed each other to ribbons."

By the time he was done reading I knew I had to do it. Still, I had no idea how he hoped to recreate such atrocities or how I was going to handle it, but if I loved him I knew I had to try. That's when he told me about his idea for the box.

"The Box" was a pine coffin that Kenyatta purchased from the local mortuary. It was four feet wide, three feet deep, and six feet long. Kenyatta bought several lengths of chain and a few thick metal loops that he screwed into the wooden floor trusses in the basement ceiling. He then connected the chains to it and, after screwing several other eyelets into the coffin, suspended the entire thing three feet off the floor. He kept the chains long and loose so that the slightest vibration caused the entire thing to sway. Then he hooked up a motor to it that pulled the pulley's up and down, rocking the box steadily like the motion of calm waves gently rocking a boat.

"This will make it feel like you're at sea. I can't exactly hire a bunch of naked Africans to pack you in here with, so this coffin will simulate that same claustrophobic feeling they must have had being packed in tight with hundreds of other slaves. I'm gonna put heaters all around the room and a humidifier to make it as hot down here as it was between decks with no windows or ventilation. It's gonna be miserable as hell. But just remember that no matter how horrible and uncomfortable it gets in there, no matter how fucked up and cruel I might seem for putting you through this, remember that it's nothing compared to what my ancestors endured. They had no safe word."

"Okay. I'll do it."

"You're gonna have to quit your job. Take a leave of absence or something. Just tell them it's for personal reasons. They won't ask questions. Then come right back here and we'll start this shit. I love you, baby. I really do. But I'm warning you that once this begins I'm fully committed. I'll become your oppressor and I won't show you any pity. No mercy. Not for four hundred days. And this box is just the beginning. My ancestor's journey through the Middle Passage was just the first part of a fucked up odyssey that lead right up to today. I'm talking about four hundred days experiencing all the hardships my people have endured for the last four hundred years. You sure you can do this?"

"I'm sure."

"I'm not gonna take it easy on you. You have your safe word if you decide you can't take it anymore, but if you do go through with it. If you last all four hundred days..."

He pulled out a small ring box and lifted the lid slowly, staring at my face, waiting to see my reaction. It was an engagement ring. A princess-cut diamond, at least two carats, with a platinum band and two smaller diamonds inset on either side. It was beautiful.

"You make it through this shit and I'll know that you really understand what it's like, what my people have gone through, what I go through every day. I'll know you're more than just some freaky redneck bitch with a low self-esteem who got tired of the white trash she's been dealing with all of her life. That you didn't just get bored and decide to try something a little kinky and go slumming with the jiggaboos. I'll know you really do love me and understand me. Then we can be together as man and wife. Then every time some sista looks at you wrong and starts in with that bullshit of you not ever being able to really understand a black man or black people, you'll know different because you can say that you've been through everything we have."

Somehow it all made sense when he put it like that. He had that way of stating things so they sounded perfectly reasonable no matter how fucked they really were, rationalizing his bullshit so well he could persuade you into doing just about anything. The way he put it, made it sound like climbing into that box was the most noble thing I could do. Like it would be insensitive if I didn't. I almost felt like if I wasn't willing to subject myself to all of this then that would somehow make me a racist or at the very least a coward. Besides, we'd already taken our S&M play to extremes I never would have imagined before I met him. He had taught me to enjoy things that would have repulsed me just months ago. How much worse could this be? I felt like I could endure anything. And then there was the ring. I'd dreamed about marrying Kenyatta many, many times, even before we'd started dating, but it was always just a childish fantasy that I'd put out of my mind almost as fast as it entered. I'm not the kind of girl that men marry, especially not men like Kenyatta who can have any woman they want. Just mentioning the possibility that he and I could someday be together forever, just the fact that he would even consider it made it impossible for me to say no.

"I'll do it."

That was two weeks ago to the day.

Perspiration ran in a constant deluge from my brow down my face. I blinked tiny droplets of sweat out of my eyes. Salty rivulets made their way to the corners of my mouth and I licked them from my lips, trying to quench my thirst. It would be hours before I could drink again. Kenyatta worked eight hours every day and sometimes nine or ten. Then he would go to the gym for another two hours. That meant I was sometimes locked in my box for twelve hours at a time. Most days he came home on his lunch break to feed me or else he dropped by on his way to the gym. But some days he left me in there without food or water or a bathroom until he came home for the night.

The heat was the worst thing at first. I was constantly sweating. My skin stuck to the damp wood and between that and the chains, every movement abraded more skin. The heat and humidity made it so hard to breathe I inevitably began to panic and claw at my box, trying to free myself, which made it sway violently and began a new problem. Seasickness. I tried to lie still, but the way he had the box hung from the center rather than the ends, the slightest shift in position sent the box tilting and reeling. Between the heat and the claustrophobia, it was too much. I could feel the gorge rising in my stomach, the bile scalding the back of my throat. Many days, as I lay interred in my coffin breathing my own funk and swaying back and forth, I was overcome with nausea and regurgitated, leaving me no choice but to lie in my own vomit for hours until Kenyatta returned. The liquefied chunks of squash and horse beans would slowly curdle in the heat, filling the boiling air with its repugnant stench until I vomited again and again, the nausea magnified by the smell of my own waste. I didn't want to go through that again. I tried to suck the scalding bile rising in my throat back down into my stomach and lie steady to quiet the swaying of the box. It worked for a while at least.

The thirst came almost immediately. From the moment the box is closed, the need for a cool drink becomes an insistent preoccupation. At first it is merely the need for some refreshment against the oppressive heat and the stench of my own sweat and funk and breath trapped in this confined space. Then, as more and more of my fluids escaped through my sweat glands, the need for liquids turned into a raging, maddening thirst. I began to count the seconds, minutes, hours until Kenyatta returned. He was all I could think about. My life revolved around him now. Without him food, water, air, sunlight, freedom did not exist. I distracted myself from my thirst, imagining the feel of his granite chest and arms as he pulled me tight against him. I imagined the feel of his cock inside me and his lips upon mine. I clenched and unclenched my Kegel muscles trying to bring myself to orgasm without using my hands and making the box sway as I fantasized about Kenyatta fucking me again. I came, a small quiet orgasm that still caused the box to tilt and sway as I imagined Kenyatta holding me in his arms face to face, lifting me off the floor while still inside of me, sliding me up and down on his cock with my full weight supported on his arms. Then I laid there quietly with the heat and the thirst rushing back in to remind me where I was.

Hours went by. I estimated that it had been about five hours, fourteen minutes, and twenty-five seconds since my master left. I was hungry and thirsty and hot and I needed to pee. That was yet another constant torment. It seems I always had to pee. I don't know where my body found the moisture with all the fluids I was constantly perspiring. But every day I went through the discomfort of holding my urine for hours waiting for my master to return so that I could use the toilet and most days I failed and relieved myself in the box. The smell of urine, added to all the other bodily odors boiling in the cramped wooden box, increased the feeling of claustrophobia and my own misery until I felt like I was going to lose my mind. The air soon became so repugnant with odors that it was impossible to breathe yet I had no choice. I sat there fighting nausea and counting down the remaining hours until my master's return.

Two hours later, I threw up. The smells and the seasickness were finally too much and I vomited up my breakfast and nearly choked on it. I rolled over in the casket as I continued to regurgitate and the swaying of the box caused it all to drip down until I was covered from head to toe in my own vomit. That's when my master finally returned. I was ashamed when he opened the box and I saw that look of disgust on his beautiful face. I hid my face in my hands and sobbed uncontrollably. I thought about saying the safe word for the first time, but I knew I wouldn't. It had only been two weeks and I would have felt like a failure. Besides, there was no way I could have brought myself to say that word.

Kenyatta hauled me out of the box and washed me off. I didn't look at him the entire time, not wanting to see the disgust on his face again. I kept my head hung low and my eyes on the floor as he hosed me off. I started crying again as I watched him hose out my box, wrinkling his nose at the smell. He filled a bucket with water and I knelt down on all fours and lapped it up like a dog. Then he brought down a bowl of overcooked horse beans with a few bits of pork in it and some rice. I was full when he finally put me back into the box, and I was petrified that I would throw up again and be left to wallow in my own filth for another two hours.

"Please. Please don't put me back in the box! Please. Just stay with me. Please!"

"You can't speak English yet remember? You'll have to be punished for that when I return."

He shut the lid to the box, padlocked it and left. I started to cry again. It seemed like another eternity went by before he returned. My mind turned inward and began to devour itself. I thought about Kenyatta at the gym, working out, making his beautiful body even more perfect while I became even more repulsive. I replayed that look of revulsion on his face when he opened the box to find me there covered in my own vomit. I moaned out loud, wishing I had the means to kill myself. I began to wonder if he was really at the gym, whether he might be seeing another woman. Rage seethed within me as I thought about him fucking some slut, sharing that wonderful cock with someone else while I was here suffering for him. I tried to push the thought out of my head, but it wouldn't go.

Why wouldn't he fuck someone else? Men are men, and after he's seen me like this he probably thinks I'm too disgusting to fuck. He can't have any respect for me. I'm just his slave, his property. Maybe he doesn't even love me? I'm a fucking fool! How did I let myself get talked into this?

Another hour went by and I started to think about my own safety. I wondered if he had remembered to lock the front door. I wondered if he had locked the basement door. I imagined I heard a window sliding open, footsteps creeping coyly across the floor above. I wondered what a burglar would do if he found me chained up like this. I began to panic. As I hyperventilated inside my stifling, oppressively hot coffin, I wondered what would happen if I had a heart attack or some other medical emergency while I was locked in the box and Kenyatta was off at the gym or fucking some whore or whatever he was doing. My panic turned to sheer terror. By the time I heard Kenyatta's keys in the basement door, I was crying hysterically. I threw myself into his arms when he released me from my box.

Kenyatta didn't push me away this time. He didn't yell or strike me or scold me. He lifted me from the box, having no trouble managing my weight even with forty pounds of iron chain added to it. He carried me up the stairs and into his bedroom. He laid me on his bed and then reached into his pocket for the key to my chains. He kissed each wrist as he unshackled me and then did the same as he unchained my ankles and then finally the thick collar around my neck. I was surprised by how gentle he was. He kissed the scabbed and torn flesh around my neck and licked the blood that trickled there. Then he kissed my lips deeply and passionately stealing the breath from my lungs.

"I love you, Kenyatta."

He smiled at me with his perfect white teeth and then stood up from the bed and walked into the bathroom. I heard him run a bath and my heart sang. I hadn't had a bath in so long it was little more than a distant memory from a lifetime ago. He lit scented candles and filled the bath with lavender oil. Then he came back for me and lowered me slowly into the steaming water. The heat burned my welts and scars and I let out a tiny yelp. As my body began to adjust to the temperature, and the warmth seeped into my tired muscles, I laid my head back with a sigh. I watched

Kenyatta undress in front of me and I felt like I was in a dream. This was all so far removed from the horrible day I'd spent in the box, nauseated and miserable. I looked around the room at the candles, the wonderful scented bubbles, and then back at Kenyatta as he shrugged himself out of his underwear and stood up. His pecs, shoulders, and biceps were swollen from exertion. Veins stood out everywhere, rushing blood to his overworked muscles. I always loved the way he looked after a hard workout, when his muscles were still all pumped up like that. I wanted him so badly. He looked magnificent.

I held out my arms and he took them and stepped into the bath with me. He sat behind me and soaped my back and shoulders, kissing and massaging as he cleaned the day's filth from my pores. He washed my arms, caressing them lovingly, and then my breasts, gently rubbing and pinching my nipples until they were hard and I was ready to explode. Then he told me to stand and he washed my legs, my ass, and between my thighs, cleaning everything thoroughly but gently. When I was completely clean, he sat me down on the edge of the tub and spread my legs.

He began by kissing my knees. I shivered as his hot breath traveled along the tender flesh of my inner thighs. Then I moaned as he licked the bathwater from my skin working his way down my thighs to where they joined at the center of me. He rubbed his cheek against my pubic hair like a kitten and I purred. Then he slid his tongue inside of me and I gasped. He made love to me with his mouth, twirling and flicking his tongue across my clitoris then sucking and nipping at it until I felt like screaming, like dying, as if I had already died and been reborn in some paradise of sin. His tongue plunged inside me again and I arched my spine and thrust my hips forward, grabbing the back of his head to thrust him in deeper. I felt him inside of me, wet and slippery as he fucked me with his tongue. My legs began to shake. He withdrew and sucked my clit into his mouth, flicking his tongue over it and swirling it around as he had once commanded me to do to his cock. I did scream then as a cataclysmic eruption tore through me and my body trembled, jerked, bucked and shook with one orgasm after another. I held his head there, pushing his face into my sex with both hands as he continued licking and sucking until one orgasm melded into the next and soon climax after climax tumbled down over one another and my body was undulating and convulsing spasmodically as if I were having a seizure. It became too much, I tried to push him away, but he wrapped his arms around my thighs and began to lick more furiously. I came again and again, pain and discomfort mixing with a pleasure that was almost too much to bear. Kenyatta could turn anything into a kind of torture, even this. Every moment with him was extreme. I screamed again, and my body seized, every muscle tense and vibrating as one final orgasm shook me to my soul.

Kenyatta rose from between my thighs and kissed my lips. Then he stood me up again on legs still quivering from the most powerful orgasms I'd ever had in my life. He turned me around and I felt his wet kisses and steamy breath on my buttocks. His tongue traced the crack of my ass and my legs trembled again. Then his tongue was inside me. He fucked my ass with his long slippery tongue and it was the most incredible sensation I'd ever felt. I came immediately. Once again reaching around to grab his head and pull him in deeper. My legs gave out and I collapsed back into the tub, trembling everywhere.

Kenyatta lifted me from the bath and stood me on a towel in the bathroom. He dried me off with one of the big cashmere towels that hung on a bar above the tub, embroidered with his initials. Once again he kissed each spot as he wiped it dry, starting from my feet, kissing each toe and then to my ankles and calves, twirling his tongue over my calf muscles and flicking it in the hollow behind each knee. He kissed his way up my thighs and I surprised myself by wanting him again. He kissed my pubic hair and then dried it before kissing it again and sliding his tongue inside me quickly. He turned me around and dried my ass, kissing each cheek. Then he kissed his way up my spine wiping away both the bathwater and his own saliva as he made his way to the back of my neck and then down the front of me, rubbing his face between my breasts and sucking each nipple. He kissed his way back down my belly and then he stood and kissed my face. He licked the bathwater from my eyelids and then from my lips and cheeks. Then he dried off my face.

Kenyatta lifted me into his arms and carried me back to his bed and laid me down on my stomach. He filled his palms with a mixture of rosewater and almond oil and began massaging me. From the bath, the sex, and now the massage, my body was completely relaxed when he slipped inside me. We made love gently and passionately with him saying all the things with his body he wouldn't have ever put into words. Then he began massaging me again. Once I was completely covered in scented oils from head to toe, he took out a powder puff and gently dusted me with some scented talc that made my skin look even whiter than it was. Then he spritzed me with perfume and stood back to admire his work.

"You are beautiful."

I felt perfect at that moment. Perfectly safe, perfectly comfortable, perfectly appreciated, perfectly loved by my perfect man.

"Stay right there."

Kenyatta stepped into his walk-in closet and came back with the full-length white chinchilla coat he'd bought me for my birthday along with the diamond studded cat collar, a leash and a pair of black leather hip boots. He bought me the outfit after our first visit to the Society of "O"—one of the oldest and largest BDSM groups in the country. He took me to one of their parties just a few weeks after we'd started dating to introduce me to the lifestyle he was already well acquainted with. That first trip all we did was watch as doms and their slaves played in the many different themed rooms of the dungeon where the event was held. We watched as men and women were whipped, branded, pierced, paddled, and cut, and we watched them fuck in every imaginable coupling from hetero to homosexual to bi-sexual threesomes and outright orgies. The only rule seemed to be that no bodily fluids could be exchanged and so latex and lubricant flowed freely.

I had never even heard of places like that then. It was all so wild and dangerous and fascinating and forbidden to me, so sexy. It surprised me to see how unimpressed Kenyatta seemed by it all. I could only imagine what his sexual history must have been like.

"How long have you known about this place?"

"I was about twenty years old the first time I came here. I was dating a woman who was much older than me, and she used to read a lot of S&M erotica, but she'd never tried it so we decided to try it together. I was down for anything back then and the kinkier the better. I wanted to do it all. We found this place together in the back of an S&M magazine. Back then, you couldn't just pay a cover charge and walk in like you can now. Everybody had to have a membership and all the members were pre-screened with an interview and not everyone got accepted. They tried hard to keep the most dangerous perverts out along with weirdos who wanted different things than they offered. I remember waiting by the phone to hear if we'd made it and then getting our membership cards in the mail. We rushed right out to the dungeon that night. We fell into our roles of top and bottom right away."

"Top and bottom?"

"Dominant and submissive, master and slave. One of the regulars showed me how to use a cat, and I hung Toni up on that rack right there and whipped her ass red."

His eyes were wistful as he reminisced and a twinge of jealousy struck me out of nowhere. I hated to think about him enjoying any pleasure with someone else that I hadn't given him. I wanted to experience everything with him.

"Why don't you strap me up there?"

"Not yet. Some other day. It's your first time. Let's just look around."

I was disappointed, but I knew even then not to say anything about it. It would have only led to a fight, which would have led to Kenyatta not speaking to me for days until he felt I'd been punished enough, so I allowed myself to be talked out of it. Besides, he was right. There was so much to see.

He said he didn't want to rush me into anything. I suspected he had other motives. He wanted to give me time to fantasize about it, to obsess over it, and eventually, to beg him for it.

"This whole lifestyle is pretty intense. It might turn you off and I don't want you to get turned off by me because of all of this. I'm not done having fun with you yet. Or you might get really into it. This scene can get really addictive. There was a time when I was here every night with a different sub. That was years ago though. Why don't you take your time and think about if this is really something you want to get into."

"Can't we just try it a little just to see if I like it?"

"I don't do anything halfway. You should know that by now. It's all or nothin' darlin'."

We walked through more rooms where couples partied in more and more intricate ways. We watched a gay couple brand each other's cocks. We paused for a moment to watch a lesbian threesome using huge dildos and some type of electric cattle prod on each other. We watched a scarification with a tall gorgeous black woman carving on an old white woman's back and rubbing what Kenyatta explained to me were ashes into the cuts to make some Wiccan occult design of raised welts.

"Is that permanent?"

"Very."

Each new room revealed something even more bizarre. We saw an old man wearing a saddle while a young dark haired woman in latex rode his back and striped his buttocks with a buggy whip. We entered a room that was humid with female musk and the scent of Astroglide, several women and even a few men were sitting around the room strapped into bizarre machines that looked like dentist chairs with dildos attached to some bicycle looking apparatus so that they fucked who ever sat on the seat as they peddled. Kenyatta laughed and shook his head. I was happy that he found the scene as ridiculous as I did.

We were still laughing as Kenyatta dragged me into a room where some sort of swap meet was going on. We picked through all kinds of S&M paraphernalia, whips and paddles and flails and cat-o'-nine-tails, dildos, vibrators, collars, and restraints of every variety and description. He bought me the studded collar that night along with the hip boots and some latex lingerie and we'd gone home and fucked like maniacs. The coat came much later. He presented it to me as a gift, but I could tell even then that it was part of *his* fantasy. Every time I wore it he made me wear the collar and the hip boots with it and either lingerie or some tight slinky dress or nothing at all if we were going to an S&M event. I figured we must be going to something like that now. I was excited, because for us it was a return to normalcy.

"Get dressed. We're going out."

"Really? Where?"

"My ancestors never knew where they were going, neither should you."

My heart sank, and the fear I'd been feeling for the last two weeks, ever since our experiment began, came rushing back. I'd almost forgotten about our little game, but he obviously had not. I looked at the coat and the boots and collar and wondered how this could possibly fit in with the oppression of black people. I couldn't imagine what he had planned for me this time and not knowing made it seem all the more terrifying. I tried to tell myself he wouldn't have been so sweet to me and made love to me so lovingly and passionately if he were going to do something terrible to me. He wouldn't have bathed me and perfumed me.

"I said get dressed. Now. We can't be late."

I took the boots from his hands, slid them on, and zipped them up. Then I took the diamond collar and fastened it around my throat. I stood and Kenyatta handed me my coat. The silk lining felt luxurious after feeling nothing but iron and wood for the last fourteen days. I ran my hands over the soft fur. It felt amazing. I felt beautiful and sexy and I could tell by the look in Kenyatta's eyes he thought I did as well.

I remembered how he made love to me that first night after he'd bought me the coat. He wouldn't let me take it off and he made me sleep at the foot of the bed curled up at his feet after he was done. The next morning he served me breakfast out of a pet dish with a saucer of milk beside it and made me crawl on my hands and knees and lap the milk from the bowl. It turned him on so much that he stood above me masturbating as I lapped up the milk and then ordered me to give him head. He came almost immediately and I lapped his cum from the head of his cock as it spurted out all over me. I licked every drop from his shaft and then licked my lips clean and purred. That's when he started calling me Kitten.

Kenyatta hooked a choke collar around my neck and attached the leash to that. Then he made me stand still as he dressed. He wore a dark suit with a black turtleneck that made him look absolutely sinister. I loved that outfit. He wore it mostly when we were going to S&M events. He added a pair of dark sunglasses that enhanced the sinister look. The combined effect made him look like a mafia hit-man and helped him to stand out among the other leather-clad doms at the Society of "O." When he was finished dressing, he led me out of the bedroom and down the stairs. I wanted to ask him again where we were going, but instead I hung my head and shuffled obediently behind him, following wherever I was led.

We climbed into his car, a black Chrysler 300 with limo tinted windows, and sped off in silence. It felt great to be outside after what seemed like endless days in the stifling heat and darkness of the basement. I watched the city rush by with a feeling of exhilaration. I almost didn't care what lay ahead, the bath, the perfume, the sex, the massage and now the feel of the luxurious fur against my bare skin and the sight and sounds of the city as it rushed by my window, made me dizzy with joy. I felt incredible.

We pulled up outside the small art gallery that I knew had a rather extensive dungeon in the rooms above where the Society of "O" held its events, and I relaxed. This was more normalcy. Whatever Kenyatta had planned, it could be no worse than a little harmless sex-play. The Society of "O" was about as safe and sane as S&M could get, so I knew he couldn't do anything too vicious, not without losing his membership and getting himself kicked out. And there was no pain or humiliation he could put me through in there that could be worse than what I'd already endured in the box. Or so I thought.

Kenyatta pulled the car around back and turned off the engine. Then he once again pulled out the book that had become his bible on how to treat me in our new roles, *400 Years of Oppression*. A shiver went through me. Still, I remained confident that, whatever he was planning, I could endure. When he started to read and the realization of what he planned to do hit me, I began to cry.

"When the slave ships arrived in America, those slaves that survived the trip and had not committed suicide, been murdered by the crew or by other desperate slaves, or succumbed to suffocation or disease, were taken off the ship and placed in a pen. There they would be washed and their skin covered with dark grease or tar to give their complexion a healthier hue and hide cuts and scars that would lessen their value. Scars upon a slave's back were considered evidence of a rebellious or unruly spirit, and would negatively impact his or her value at auction. The slaves were then branded with a hot iron to identify them as property before being removed from the pen one by one and made to stand on a makeshift stage so they could be seen by potential bidders. Before the bidding began, prospective buyers were allowed onto the platform to inspect the merchandise prior to purchase. The slaves had to endure being poked, prodded and forced to open their mouths and show their teeth and gums the way horses and cattle are inspected before being sold at market. The auctioneer would set a minimum bid for each slave, higher for fit, young slaves and lower for older, very young, or sickly slaves. Then the bidding would begin.

"They would be made to hold up their heads and prance briskly back and forth, while customers would feel their hands and arms and bodies, make them do turns, and sometimes even calisthenics and acrobatics to display their physical fitness.

"Heartbreaking scenes of husbands and wives being sold to separate masters, sons and daughters sold away from their parents, and families split up forever were commonplace. Not understanding what was transpiring, the African slaves would beg and plead, crying and screaming in panic as their families were torn apart. The utter misery of seeing those you loved taken away by hostile foreign hands while you sit powerless to save them, seeing your spouse, your children, your mothers and fathers, pulled from your gasp never to be seen again, is unimaginable. The shocked and terrified faces of children torn from their parent's embrace and handed into the arms of their new masters were utterly heartbreaking as were the tears and desperate embraces of husbands and wives saying goodbye for the last time as they were sold to different masters."

I was wailing uncontrollably by the time he was finished reading. It didn't take a genius to figure out what Kenyatta was planning to do, but even as his intentions became clear to me, I couldn't believe it, couldn't accept that he would do such a thing, that he would take it this far.

"No, Master! No! Please! Please don't sell me! Please, don't give me away. I'll be good. I swear I'll do whatever you want! I'll never complain! I'll do anything. Please don't sell me. Please!"

I was in a panic. The thought of being handed into the arms of another master had never occurred to me. That Kenyatta would sell me like I was little more than property was something I would have never considered.

"Don't speak again or I'll have to punish you."

"Please, Kenyatta...I mean...M-Master! You can beat me! You can whip me as hard as you like! Please, baby! Please I don't want to leave you! Please don't send me away!"

"All you have to do is say the safe word if you want it to stop. But this is what my ancestors went through, being sold away from their loved ones, sold to strangers they knew nothing about, some who were inhumanly cruel. Watching their wives and children torn from them and given to strange white people to do God knows what with them. Most of them didn't even understand what was happening or why. That's what they had to go through and that's what you're going to go through unless you want it to stop now? Unless you want to say the safe word and end this? Then we can go our separate ways right now. Your choice. Either way you lose me."

I thought about it then, saying that word. I thought about giving up and seeing that disappointed and disgusted look in Kenyatta's eyes as he walked away forever.

"I won't say it. I'm still going through with it."

Kenyatta nodded his approval, still looking at me with suspicion. He grabbed my leash and pulled me forward.

"Then no more crying. No more begging. You go in there and you do whatever I say without question. You get up there on that auction block and you smile your lily white ass off and you obey."

He jerked my choke chain as he spoke, dragging me out of the car. I never had an opportunity to reply but none was necessary. He knew I'd obey.

Kenyatta walked me to the back door of the art gallery, jerking my choke chain every now and again to keep me moving. Beyond the door was a long flight of stairs that led to the huge loft above where the festivities took place. A big hairy leatherman stood at the top of the stairs looking like a Hell's Angel except for the leather chaps he wore with no jeans underneath so that his genitals were freely exposed. He wore a spiked leather cock ring so that he maintained a painful-looking erection. It was already turning purple, and I wondered how long it had been that way. The look was completed by a leather vest with no shirt. Both his cock and his nipples were pierced. He had a thick beard speckled with gray and he wore a spiked dog collar around his neck. His chest, arms, and shoulders were enormous like a powerlifter and his hairy belly was proportionately just as large. He looked like he could have snapped my neck with one hand, but Kenyatta still towered over him when he stood next to him. Attached to the dog collar was a long chain and holding the end of the chain was a thin and strikingly beautiful middle-aged woman with a full head of gray hair that hung to her waist. She wore a red leather bustier and corset, a long black leather skirt, and red leather boots ending in spiked stiletto heels that were at least six-inches long. Her eye-makeup was dramatic, dark eye shadow and eyeliner, burgundy rouge to make her sharp cheekbones appear almost cadaverous and deep red lipstick. Despite all of that, she managed to look somewhat pleasant and even friendly as she asked for our membership cards.

Kenyatta reached into his jacket to retrieve his wallet and the woman laughed.

"I'm just kidding with you, King. Everybody knows you. It's forty dollars tonight for the auction. It's a charity event. Unless you've brought us something to auction off?"

She reached out and opened my coat so that my nude body was fully exposed to both her eyes and those of her big hairy sub. That's how it was at this place sometimes. Once they knew you were a sub, every dom in the place acted like they owned you. I hated that, and I knew it bothered Kenyatta too. So I was surprised when he said nothing as the woman ran her hands over my breasts down my stomach and reached around and patted me on my ass.

"She's lovely. Is she trained?"

Her eyes narrowed in on the collar pinching into the raw skin around my throat. Unlike the auctions that took place centuries ago when the slaves came over from Africa, my wounds would increase my selling price. A sub who'd already been trained by a respected dom was highly valued in the S&M community and Kenyatta, or King as they knew him in the scene, was very well-known and well-respected I had learned.

"Of course, she is."

"Mmmmm, wonderful. So, is she for sale?"

"The minimum bid has to be at least five-hundred. She's not like the used up tired old bottoms you guys usually drag up on stage. This one is newly trained."

I wanted to cry again as I watched him write the nickname he'd given to me down on the auction list. "Kitten." It took everything I had to hold the tears in.

"She'll probably go for twice that. I might even bid on her myself. Just go in and march her up on stage. We'll be starting in a minute. I'm closing the door at ten o'clock. I don't want to miss the auction either. I am sponsoring the thing."

We walked in and I stared at the familiar decor, which now looked foreign and hostile to me. The whipping post and crucifix in the center of the room, the rack on the wall by the windows, the dentist chair and the enormous canopy bed, twice the size of a California King, that sat in the far corner with what looked like over a dozen people crowded onto it. All eyes were pointed to the stage where the slaves were being prepared for auction. My heart rose up into my throat as Kenyatta marched me up there under the lights. He pushed me out among the other slaves and then ripped the fur coat from my shoulders leaving me completely nude and exposed under the stage lights. There was a gasp from the crowd and then applause. I tried to cover myself, but Kenyatta ordered me to stand at attention and I obeyed. He then told me to walk back and forth across the stage with the other slaves. Again, I did as I was told.

The stage lights turned red and the pulsing techno music thundering through the loft faded out, leaving only the hollow sound of shuffling feet and a few scattered applause. A huge leather dyke, the female equivalent of the big biker guarding the door, strode up on stage with a bullwhip in one hand and a microphone in the other. Her makeup was just as severe as the woman who ran the place, dark eye shadow smeared from her eyelids almost to her temples and a thick bead of eyeliner surrounded each emerald green eye. Her lips were large and pouty as if they'd been injected with collagen but one look at her belied such vanity. A thick nest of flaming red hair was knotted into a tight bun on top of her head and her mammoth breasts were squeezed into a tight corset and lifted up to her neckline, still managing to undulate and giggle with each step despite their bondage. The woman somehow managed to be beautiful, even sexy, despite her titanic girth. The entire crowd fell silent in anticipation as she cleared her throat and began to announce the show.

"Good evening subs and doms, sadists and masochists, I am Mistress Delia. Welcome to our sixteenth quarterly charity slave auction benefiting the AIDS Research Foundation. I hope you brought a lot of money because we've got some top quality flesh to auction off tonight! The rules are simple. Anyone wishing to bid must purchase bondage bills from Lady "O" at the front at the price of ten dollars for every hundred. This is a charity event so five dollars of every ten you spend will go to The AIDS Research Foundation. Our lovely slaves will be brought up one-by-one onto the stage and anyone wishing to may come up to the front of the stage for a closer inspection. Once the bidding begins, you will have twenty seconds to make a counter bid or the highest bid wins. Some of the slaves tonight will be yours for the evening and some for much, much longer depending on the contract they or their owners have signed. Remember that this is just a fantasy auction however, and these slaves do have the right to refuse to go with you even after you have purchased them. That does not however mean that you get your money back. We have a few one-year contracts for sale and even a lifetime contract or two. The minimum bid for any slave is one hundred dollars though some may be higher depending on the slave's youth, beauty, and overall pedigree. So get those dollars ready! I'll give you a few moments to purchase your bondage bills up at the front while we finalize a few contracts and then the bidding will begin with our first slave!"

I trembled as I heard the words "lifetime contract." I held out hope that Kenyatta would only sell me away for one night and not to be someone's permanent slave. I knew that I could still refuse to leave with my new master even after I was sold, but I wasn't sure how Kenyatta would respond to my refusal. There were so many thoughts going through my head when Mistress Delia approached us and asked us what type of contract we were selling. I looked at Kenyatta, pleading with him silently. I wanted to cry and beg and scream, but I knew how much that would have embarrassed him. He would have never forgiven me for it. So, instead I sat silently as Kenyatta took the clip board from Mistress Delia's large meaty hands with the painted nails so long that they curled at the ends, and began to fill it out while I strained to see which box he checked.

"You look stunning tonight, Delia. Do you still switch? I'd love to play with you again sometime."

"That is so tempting. You don't know how tempting, really, but I'm afraid me and my new sub are in a monogamous relationship. But maybe she'd be cool with it if you could take us both on?"

"Now, that would be fun. Remember though, I'm not just about whipping and spanking. I fuck whoever I top. Does your new playmate like dick?"

"Don't let the hype fool you. Most lesbians like dick every now and again. It's just what's attached to it that turns us off. That's why we opt for vibrating plastic instead. Besides, then we can pick the size that best suits us whereas with men you're stuck with what you got and most men aren't built like you, darlin'. I'll definitely keep your offer in mind though. I'm sure we could work something out."

They talked about fucking each other as if I wasn't even standing there, and my jealousy was raging. I wanted to claw the bitch's eyes out, but Kenyatta had trained me too well. I stood there obediently with my head down, watching as Kenyatta made small talk with the huge lesbian while I waited to see whether I was losing him forever or just for the evening.

"How big are those magnificent tits of yours anyway, Delia?" Kenyatta asked hefting them in both hands while still holding pen and paper.

"I'm an F-cup if you must know," Delia replied, sticking her massive breasts out proudly.

"My God, woman, I didn't even know they came that big."

"I was a G-cup before I lost weight."

"I could lose myself between those tits. Definitely call me."

Kenyatta casually checked off lifetime membership in the middle of his playful flirtation and handed the form back to Delia as if he'd done nothing more significant than sold her a box of Girl Scout cookies. I wanted to scream, but again I remained silent as the man I loved prepared to give me away to another.

Mistress Delia, stomped back onto the stage in her size ten stiletto hip boots, carrying the contracts for the dozen or more slaves up for bid. I looked around me at the other slaves who were about to be auctioned. They ranged in age from retirees to kids just barely old enough to legally drink. Some of them were new to the scene, novice subs in search of their first master. Some of them were veterans who'd been topped by almost every dom in the scene at one time or another. Predictably, there were more gay males than females and more of the jaded old bottoms than fresh-faced newbies. They all appeared anxious and excited. A few of them even looked bored. I was perhaps the only depressed and terrified face in the crowd. I was the only one who didn't want to be there.

"Isn't this exciting?" a young Filipino kid asked in a voice that was annoyingly bubbly, almost giddy. I turned my back on him and lowered my head to hide the sudden burst of tears. I moved closer to Kenyatta and leaned on him as I wept, hiding my tears in his chest.

"Please, Master. Please don't sell me. Please don't give me away," I whispered to him as I wept.

Kenyatta removed a handkerchief from his suit jacket and dabbed it in the tears, wiping them from my eyes then he kissed me gently on each cheek.

"No more of that. Don't embarrass me tonight. Go out there and show them what a well-trained, disciplined slave you are."

I could tell that he was nervous. He didn't know what I'd do. He was afraid I'd embarrass him, get out there and fall apart, maybe start screaming and crying, fighting all the way to the stage. Or maybe he was afraid I'd run off the stage and refuse to go with whoever purchased me. That was my right, but it would be his shame. The other jealous doms who were intimidated by his comparative youth, good looks, and statuesque physique would laugh at him behind his back and gossip non-stop for years. I sucked up my tears and calmed myself. I could never embarrass him like that. I looked over at him and let him see the resolve in my face. He smiled at me and my heart felt as if it was pumping razor blades. My bottom lip trembled and my knees shook. Tears welled up in my eyes and it took everything within me to keep them from spilling out as I looked at his handsome face and that beautiful smile and the thought crossed my mind that I might never see him again or not at least until the 400 days was up. I wiped the back of my hand across my eyes to catch any tears before they could fall, then I turned toward the stage. I wouldn't cry. I wouldn't make a scene. Kenyatta had trained me well and I wanted everyone to know what a great dom my master was. I was proud of him, and I wanted everyone else to be proud of him too. I wanted him to be proud of me.

Mistress Delia was back on the stage. The DJ cranked the music up a few decibels so that Delia had to

raise her voice slightly to be heard. The first slave
sauntered out with his head held high, strutting proud as
a peacock. He was young and blonde with a slight
tummy and no muscle tone. He looked like an office
executive who had just left his cubicle in time to slip the
leather gear out of his trunk and dash up onto the stage. I
could imagine what he looked like in a shirt and tie and
probably a pair of glasses that he cleaned compulsively.
I knew the type. I worked with them every day and most
of them needed a good spanking. The office boy bent
over to show his asshole which was miraculously
distended. He slipped a large butt plug in that was
roughly the circumference of a soda can and the bids
came fast and furious. He went for six hundred dollars.

Next a mountainous woman, almost as large as
Mistress Delia, walked up onto the stage and began
clipping clothes hangers all over her titanic breasts. The
bidding was slow for her. She went to the first bidder for
two hundred dollars.

A man that everyone in the scene new simply as
"Old George" walked up on stage, and I was moved into
place to follow him. Old George was well known in the
scene. At fifty-seven he was one of the oldest members
of the Society of "O" and by far the most jaded. It was
rumored that it took vise grips on his nipples and
vigorous cutting and caning to get him off. Kenyatta
once confessed that he was afraid that he had
experienced so much so early in life that he was dulling
his senses to pleasure and pain and would wind up just
like Old George when he got older. The idea terrified
him. It terrified me too. The crowd was apparently just

as intimidated by the depths of Old George's masochism because he stood up there for almost a full minute without a single bid. Finally a young dom who didn't know any better placed a mercy bid and Old George left the stage in the company of his new master for the price of fifty dollars. Then it was my turn.

Mistress Delia gestured for me to accompany her on the stage and my legs began to shake again. Every muscle locked and refused to move. The room began to rock and tilt as if I was back in my box and everything began to gray, starting to go black. The crack of a whip on my naked ass brought me back. I let out a yelp and hopped out onto the stage, turning to see Kenyatta returning the bullwhip to the amused leather dyke he'd borrowed it from.

"This beautiful sub was trained by our very own Master King. She is young and beautiful and experienced in all aspects of pain and pleasure. She enjoys spanking, caning, whipping, bondage, humiliation, and light blood play. Wow. She is quite a connoisseur for one so young. The bidding will start for this beautiful young bottom at five hundred dollars."

The bids flew as I knew they would. I was fresh meat, and I was the first sub Kenyatta had ever placed up for bid in all the years he'd been a member. He left the stage as soon as the bidding started and walked out into the crowd. My heart pounded, afraid that he was going to leave the loft with me still on stage going to the highest bidder. Instead he took a seat in the back of the room on the enormous bed, squeezed in between the other subs and doms, some of whom were already fucking. I just stared at him. Our eyes locked across the distance, and Kenyatta smiled again as the bidding quickly went from five hundred to seven hundred to a thousand and finally to two thousand.

"Two thousand going once. Two thousand going twice…"

In a panic, I looked down at the grizzled old dom who'd bid two thousand dollars for the right to torture and humiliate me. He was nearly as old as Old George and probably just as jaded and debauched. His head was shaven and his scalp was wrinkled and scarred from too much time in the sun and too many barroom brawls in his youth. He wore a black t-shirt and black jeans, and his body was thin and wrinkled but still hard and athletic. His face was lean and angular. Hard lines cut deep into the skin around his eyes and mouth and sharp cheek bones jutted through even more prominently than Kenyatta's, only on him, with his eyelids sunken deep beneath his brow, it made him look sinister and cadaverous rather than regal. His thin lips were surrounded by a goatee that was turning from gray to white. There was something cruel in his eyes that terrified me every bit as much as the thought of leaving Kenyatta. I looked back up at my master just as he raised his hand.

"Three thousand dollars."

I almost fainted. I was so overjoyed that tears leaped into my eyes and I began to laugh out loud. I didn't care that I was going back home to that little box in the basement. All I cared was that I was going home with my master. He hadn't sold me.

"Well, here's a first. Master King is bidding on his own slave. Three thousand going once. Three thousand going twice. Sold! To King for three thousand dollars. You may claim your slave, Sir," Mistress Delia pronounced with a flourish.

Kenyatta walked back across the room and up onto the stage. Everyone cheered when I ran across the stage and dove into his arms. I wept uncontrollably as he wrapped my fur coat around me once again.

"Come on, Kitten. Let's go home." He hooked his leash back onto my collar and led me from the stage as more applause rose from the audience. This was probably the most romantic thing any of these libertines had witnessed in years. I kissed my Master's full lips and stroked his powerful jaw, then ducked my head against his chest as he wrapped his powerful arm around my shoulders and whisked me from the room. We walked quickly to the exit, pausing only for Kenyatta to pay for the merchandise he had purchased.

"Well, that was quite a little show. Why would you pay for your own property? Don't tell me you're getting soft?" the middle-aged woman in the red bustier said with a sarcastic grin as Kenyatta withdrew three thousand dollars in Bondage Bucks from his pocket. Roughly the equivalent of three hundred dollars.

"It's for charity. Just having a little fun in support of a good cause."

He turned his back and we walked together down the steps and out into the parking lot with me holding tight to my master and thinking I never wanted to let him go.

We drove home in silence. I held my master the entire ride, my head nestled against his strong chest, one of his massive arms draped around my shoulders pulling me close, feeling safe and protected now that I hadn't been sold away. I had come so close to losing him that now I knew I loved him more than anything else in life. I knew now more than ever that I would do anything to keep him. He had taught me two lessons that night.

We pulled into the garage and Kenyatta hopped out and dragged me out of the car by my leash. He led me into the kitchen and I started to turn toward the basement when he jerked my leash and led me away from the basement door and toward the back yard.

Out in the yard there was a wooden shed. I couldn't remember seeing it there before, but it looked old so it must have been there all along and I had merely overlooked it. Kenyatta pulled off my fur coat and ordered me to remove the hip boots. Finally he removed the collar too and then walked back toward the house leaving me standing naked in the yard. I became self-conscious of the neighbors and looked quickly around, noting that the six foot block walls that surrounded the yard had recently been raised another three courses and were now just shy of ten feet tall. No one would be able to see into the yard now.

I turned to look at Kenyatta as he opened the patio door and stepped back into the house. He said nothing to me, did not even turn to look back at me. He closed the sliding glass door without so much as a word, leaving me standing there wondering what I was supposed to do.

I wanted to ask him if he wanted me to follow him into the house or wait for him in the yard. He had always given me instructions and now without his orders I was lost and confused. For a moment I feared that he was abandoning me. Then I reassured myself that if he was kicking me out he would have stripped me down in the front yard and kicked me to the curb. This was something else.

But what?

The patio light went out followed by the kitchen light and a few moments later the light went on in Kenyatta's bedroom. I still did not know what I was supposed to do. I could only hope that he would come back to tell me what to do. I didn't even care if he came back with the bullwhip as long as he did something, as long as he came back to me.

Was there a whipping post in the shed? Would Kenyatta come back down and take me into the shed for a good whipping with the bullwhip? But for what? I had done everything he asked me to do tonight. Was I supposed to follow him up to the bedroom?

I didn't know what to do. I stood there a while longer until the light went out in Kenyatta's bedroom. I still thought he might be coming back down the stairs with the whip so I remained standing right where he had left me until another five minutes went by and he hadn't returned. Then my own fear of someone, one of the neighbors, peeking over the wall and seeing me standing there naked, overcame me and I walked over to the shed and stepped inside.

The shed had a dirt floor with a large pile of hay stacked in the corner, a wool army blanket draped across it. There was a fireplace with wood and a cast iron pot I assumed for cooking. A hole in the ground and a bucket of water in the back of the shed was to serve as my toilet. I looked around with my mouth hanging open. I couldn't believe he had kicked me out of the house. I almost wanted to cry before I realized that this meant I was through with the box in the basement. The auction had symbolized my arrival in America and now I was at my master's house. Now, officially his property, officially a slave.

I had no idea what my duties were to be. I immediately realized just how little I knew about the life of a slave. Almost all of my knowledge had come from watching the mini-series of *Roots* on PBS. I didn't know if he was going to put me out in a field somewhere and make me pick cotton or tobacco or if he'd let me work in the big house, cooking and cleaning and doing whatever else he required of me. That night I couldn't sleep. I was too nervous and anxious, wondering what Kenyatta had planned for me next. The moon traveled from one end of the sky to the other before I finally awoke to the sound of my door being kicked open.

"Get in the kitchen and get breakfast ready. And then help mistress with her hair and makeup."

Kenyatta stood in the doorway to my little shack in his bathrobe with a toothbrush in his hand, glaring at me as if I'd failed him in some way.

Mistress? What mistress? What new ingredient had Kenyatta added to the mix? Had he brought a new woman into the house to assist in my torment and if so, was he fucking her too?

I blinked the morning sun from my eyes and stared back at him with my eyebrow raised, wondering what he was up to, then I remembered my role and lowered my head to stare at his foot, which was tapping the dirt floor impatiently as he waited for me to crawl out of bed.

Kenyatta threw some clothes at my feet as I rose from my bed, then crossed his arms over his chest, waiting for me to dress myself. Two simple dresses, one brown one gray, an apron, a pair of white stockings, and some plain brown flats. He had obviously picked them out of a thrift store somewhere because there were places where the dresses had been torn and mended. He had also purchased them very early in the experiment, before I'd lost all my weight. The clothes now hung loosely from my bony frame as I hurried to shrug my way into them while Kenyatta's eyes crawled all over me. I could tell that he wanted me, but something was holding him back.

Who was this mistress?

I didn't dare ask. I knew I'd be finding out soon.

Kenyatta smiled mischievously as he turned and walked back into the house.

I finished dressing and raced to follow him, now nearly as terrified and angry as I'd been at the auction the night before.

What woman had Kenyatta brought into the house?

I pulled open the screen door and shuffled nervously into the kitchen with my head down, but my eyes looking up and darting everywhere in search of this strange woman I was expected to serve. There was no one in the kitchen so I began pulling out the pots and pans to cook breakfast. I was taking the bacon and eggs from the refrigerator when someone smacked me hard on the ass. I jumped and one of the eggs tumbled from the carton and cracked open on the floor as I spun around.

There was a small slender black woman standing behind me dressed in a short silk robe that just barely covered her panties. Her arms were crossed over her tiny pear-shaped breasts and a sardonic grin scarred her otherwise beautiful face. Her nails were long and perfectly manicured, her toes were painted as well, her legs were slender and tone, and her skin was a flawless caramel, smooth and unblemished. With the exception of one side smashed flat from where she'd obviously slept on it, her hair still looked as if she'd just left a beauty parlor. Everything about her said "high maintenance" and I recognized her instantly even though I'd never actually met her before. She was Kenyatta's ex-wife.

"That ass ain't quite so big anymore is it? I'm sure Kenyatta must be terribly disappointed."

She looked me up and down, scowling contemptuously.

"Clean that shit up. I want my eggs over medium and my bacon extra-crisp. Oh, and hurry up and make me some coffee. Two creams one sugar."

I was still staring at her with my mouth hanging open in astonishment when she turned around and walked to the kitchen table. She sat down and crossed her legs, her robe fell open and she was almost naked beneath it. Her body was perfect, not an ounce of fat on it. Her breasts were small but round and perky with large dark nipples like Hershey's kisses. She was wearing a thong and it was obvious that she'd recently had a Brazilian wax. Looking at her it was hard to understand what Kenyatta had ever seen in me. I was this woman's exact opposite. She was hard and lean and brown; I was soft and fleshy and white, at least I was when Kenyatta had first met me, before he'd starved the pounds off of me. Every woman I knew would have killed for her body. She almost had a six-pack. But yet Kenyatta had left her for me, and now she was back and I was to be her slave as well as his.

She gestured impatiently for me to get to work, hands splayed out palms up in front of her and thrust in my direction. Then she rolled her eyes and shook her head. More so than ever I wanted to say to hell with this experiment. No man was worth this. I thought about taking off my apron and tossing it right in this bitch's face then marching right upstairs and telling Kenyatta what a cruel twisted bastard I thought he was. But I knew he'd just pull a chapter out of that damn book and make me feel like I was the one being insensitive. Plus, it would mean that I'd never be his wife, though his ex-wife being in the house called that into question for me anyway. I'd have to wait for Kenyatta to explain it to me though I suspected he wouldn't, preferring to leave me with my own fears and doubts.

Were they back together? Was he fucking her? And if they are back together then why would he continue the game? Was this just some twisted plan the two of them had all along to make me fall in love and then humiliate and embarrass me as some kind of punishment to all white people...or maybe just to punish white women who date black men? But he'd been dating me for months before the experiment began and he'd always treated me like a queen. If this was still just part of the experiment, how the hell had he gotten her to agree to it? Of all the women he could have had play this role, why her? Why not one of the dominatrices he knew from the scene?

I found myself immobilized by doubt. My head reeled from a hurricane of questions spiraling through my skull. My legs began to tremble and tears welled up in my eyes. I wanted to collapse on the floor and cry. I wanted to attack this bitch and claw her perfect face to ribbons. I wanted to walk right out the door and never look back. I wanted to marry Kenyatta. I wanted him to love me and protect me forever.

"Are you going to clean that up?" She was tapping her foot and glaring at me like she was talking to an idiot, which I must have looked like standing there in the middle of the kitchen with my mouth hanging open and a broken egg oozing around my feet.

I finally broke my stare, wiped away the tears threatening to spill, closed my gaping mouth, and turned to grab a sponge from the sink. From the corner of my eye, I could see her smiling triumphantly as I knelt before her on my hands and knees, scrubbing the floor. I almost wished I was back in the basement crammed in that little box. I had a feeling that dealing with this bitch would be much worse.

CHAPTER IV

The movie had just begun when I could feel Kenyatta's hands slide down between my legs. He masturbated me to orgasm as we watched *March of the Penguins* in the back of the theater while a classroom of eight-year-olds sat up by the screen enraptured by the sound of Morgan Freeman's voice. I collapsed into a fit of giggles as I came and hugged Kenyatta tight, smiling from ear to ear as I snuggled against his chest.

"Don't fall in love now."

It was like a splash of cold water in my face.

"What?"

"We're just having fun. Don't fall in love. I'm the wrong guy for that."

"I-I'm not falling in love."

But I was, and I was hurt and embarrassed that he had caught me at it. This was only our fifth or sixth date. Too early to be thinking about marriage and kids. Too early to start thinking that maybe he was the perfect man for me, the one I had been waiting for all my life. But I was thinking those things. Me—white-trash tough, jaded, street-smart. I had fallen for a man I barely knew in less than two weeks.

"Yes you are."

He winked at me, then turned back to the screen as if he really gave a fuck about those damned penguins.

"Fuck you, Kenyatta. You're an asshole!"

"Yeah. I may be. But you're still in love with me."

I didn't know what to say and so I continued to stare at the movie as the penguins marched across the screen and some little kid in the front row spilled his popcorn and began to cry. I knew how he felt. I wanted to cry too. I also wanted to laugh and shout and make love again. I was in love!

And I still was. Even as I served this evil bitch her bacon and eggs and watched her drink her coffee, I still loved the man who had placed me in this awkward, uncomfortable position.

"These eggs taste like shit!"

Mistress tossed her entire plate onto the floor and I quickly, obediently, snatched a washrag from the sink and knelt to clean up her mess. I noted that she'd eaten most of the food on the plate before mounting her dramatic display of displeasure. She scowled down at me as I scrubbed the tile floor.

Kenyatta entered the room, dressed exquisitely in an athletic-cut black Brooks Brothers suit and a pink shirt with a black knit tie from J-Crew. He looked from his ex-wife to me, on my knees, sweeping cold eggs, bits of bacon, and shards of porcelain into my hand. Then he walked past me, over to his hateful ex-wife, and kissed her on the lips. Not a long, lingering, passionate kiss. Just a peck, but my heart sank immediately and I felt like a fool.

"Goodbye, Angela. You have a great day. I'll see you after work."

I stood up, trembling, preparing to storm out, wondering if now was the time to scream the safe word at the top of my lungs and fearing what the two of them would do to me if I did. I knew Kenyatta would have simply thrown me out, but Angela, his bitch of an ex-wife, may have attacked me. Then Kenyatta leaned in close to me and recited a few sentences, obviously memorized from the book. He whispered them to me, meaning them solely for my ears, as if we were co-conspirators or adulterers engaged in some scandalous and clandestine affair.

CHAPTER V

"Contrary to popular belief, female house-slaves were often treated worse than their counterparts in the tobacco and cotton fields. They were frequently raped by their masters and would bear the master's half-white children. These children, along with their mothers, were subject to the scorn and abuse of their half-siblings and worse, that of the mistress of the house, for whom they were a reminder of the master's infidelity. Beatings were an almost daily occurrence. Life in the house was a unique type of hell for the female house-slaves."

That's all he said, then he patted me on my greatly diminished ass and walked out the door, leaving me at the mercy of the new mistress of the house. I stood a moment, watching the door close behind him as he entered the garage. I heard him start up the Chrysler, the garage door squeal and whine as it rose then rattled back down behind him as Kenyatta exited the garage and drove to work.

"You're not done."

Angela's voice roused me from my momentary torpor. I considered Kenyatta's final words before he left. What he had set up here was no different from what his people had gone through. I couldn't give up now.

"Y-yes mistress?"

"I said, you're not done! There are still eggs all over the floor!"

I looked at the mess then slid down to my hands and knees to finish scrubbing. I scooped up the remaining eggs and shards of broken plate and dumped them in the wastebasket. When I looked behind me, Mistress was staring at me, smiling in a way that made my skin crawl. There was nothing warm or pleasant in the expression. I could almost see the loathsome thoughts slithering around behind her eyes like maggots through a corpse.

I told myself I was just overreacting, but there was cruelty and lust sparkling in her eyes like naked electricity. It was the expression I'd seen on the faces of so many men as they shouted crude seductions from passing cars and pantomimed lascivious acts they wanted to perform on me. The same expression I'd seen on the faces of men who got too grabby in bars and followed me out into the parking lot, causing me to pull the pepper spray from my purse and occasionally to actually use it. The same expression I'd seen on the faces of the men who got violent after I made the mistake of inviting them into my bed.

"Come here, white bitch," Mistress hissed.

I cringed at the sound of her hateful voice. There were a dozen vile names I wanted to call her in return, a dozen sardonic retorts. Instead, I shuffled over to her, nervously wringing my hands and staring down at her tiny pedicured feet.

"Yes, Mistress?"

"Tell me something, how did such an ugly, flabby, pale thing like you wind up with my man? Hmmm? Tell me that."

"I don't know, Mistress."

She snorted in derision.

"Go make me a fucking drink, a bloody Mary, and hurry the fuck up."

Kenyatta had chosen well for this part of the experiment. Angela didn't have to fake animosity toward me. Her enmity was genuine. I could feel it boiling off her in waves, radiating from her skin like August sunrays off asphalt. Angela was a total bitch, and I would soon discover that her imagination for cruelty went every bit as far as anything I would have expected from Kenyatta. She was heartless and she hated me. I was, after all, fucking her husband. It didn't matter that they were divorced. She had him first and, in her mind, he still belonged to her and she no doubt knew that if I could endure this trial, I'd be his new wife.

I walked into the dining room, removed a bottle from the wet bar, and poured two fingers of vodka into a glass. I added tomato juice, Worcestershire sauce, a splash of lemon, horseradish, Louisiana hot sauce, and a dash of pepper and celery salt. I was tempted to spit in it, but was afraid she was watching me somehow. I walked back into the kitchen and handed her the drink. She took a sip, closed her eyes, and let out a sigh.

"That's good."

She squinted at me as I stood there in the middle of the kitchen in my raggedy, secondhand house dress, hands clasped in front of me, eyes averted from her scrutiny.

"Why are you doing this? Do you know how crazy this shit is? Why are you letting him put you through all this bullshit? He's sick, you know that? He's a twisted motherfucker and you're a goddamn fool for putting up with all this. You should run as far away from his crazy ass as you can."

I stood there, unmoving, head bowed in supplication, not responding, holding on to the memory of that beautiful diamond ring Kenyatta held out to me the day he proposed this experiment to me.

"You're fucking pathetic, you know that? You're a disgrace to women letting a man walk over you like this."

She spit at me and I stood there and took it without flinching. Her saliva struck me in the face and oozed down my cheek. I didn't respond, didn't even bother wiping it off. I knew the sight of it would disgust her and my own unwavering obedience would frustrate her even more. My obedience would be my defiance, and she would spend every day trying to break me, trying to make me go back on my commitment to Kenyatta.

"Wipe your face."

She threw a towel at my feet. I picked it up and wiped her spittle from my face.

"Take off that dress. You want to be a slave, you're gonna get treated like a slave. Put your hands against that wall."

I complied without a word.

"You stay right the fuck there."

Doubts sprouted like dandelions in my mind, multiplying until they filled my every thought as I stood waiting for Angela to return with some new punishment. For the first time I doubted my desire to proceed with the experiment, more than my ability to endure it.

I felt the crack of the whip a split second before I heard it. It cut deep into my skin, searing into the muscle like a heated knife and sending a spray of vaporized blood into the air. I clenched my teeth and waited for the next one.

"Don't move and don't fucking turn around."

She cracked it again. It was obvious she'd used it before. You didn't crack a whip like that the first time you picked it up. I wondered how much she and Kenyatta had "played" when they were married. Maybe this is what she meant by Kenyatta being a sick freak. Maybe he had convinced her to partake in his sadistic lifestyle when they were still together and now she was experiencing some guilt over whatever she'd done. If she was, then her guilt was obviously due in part because she'd enjoyed it. I could hear her rapid breaths and it wasn't just from the exertion of wielding the lash. She was getting off on it.

The whip cracked again and I let out a whelp. The pain was intense. I had been whipped many times by Kenyatta and he had obviously taken it easy on me. I hadn't imagined there was anything gentle about the whippings, canings, and spankings I'd endured from Kenyatta, but I'd had little to compare it to. Now, I knew that he'd been holding back, because this bitch wasn't, and the pain was so intense I was having difficulty remaining standing. I felt like I was going to pass out.

Angela was breathing heavier now, she was practically panting. I heard her grunt each time she cracked the whip across my back. She was putting everything she had into each stroke, exerting herself in her effort to destroy me, but there was still something peculiar in the rhythm of her breaths. I could almost imagine her masturbating with one hand as she striped my back with bleeding welts.

The tip of the lash wrapped around my body and cut into my belly. My knees buckled. I had to hold onto the refrigerator to keep from falling. The whip cracked again and this time she wrapped the whip completely around so the tip cut into my breasts. This time I did fall. I collapsed to my knees, bleeding and sweating, trembling in agony, waiting for the next blow in silent dread, but it never came. I could still hear Angela panting heavily behind me. Finally, I dared turn to look.

Angela's robe was open and she was naked underneath. Her body was a work of art, hard, lean, shaved, glistening with a sheen of perspiration. But it wasn't her physique that caused the sharp intake of breath. Just as I had imagined, she was furiously masturbating and she was staring right at me.

"Come here, bitch."

I guessed bitch was my new name. I did as commanded and crawled over to her on my hands and knees. I was still in agony from the whipping and could not have walked if I wanted to. Angela was still fingering her swollen clit unselfconsciously. She sat down at the kitchen table, turned the chair so she was facing me and threw one of her legs up on the table, baring her sex to me. She beckoned me forward.

"I said come here. Get over here!"

I crawled closer and she took her finger out of her pussy and rubbed it against my lips.

"Open your mouth."

I opened my mouth and she slid her finger, wet with her vaginal juices, between my lips. Obediently, I sucked her finger clean. I thought I could taste Kenyatta's semen inside of her. I was probably imagining it, but I wouldn't have put it past either of them. She had fucked him and she wanted me to know it.

"You like how I taste, bitch?"

I didn't answer. I didn't know what to say.

"Lick my pussy."

I knew it was coming, but it was still shocking to hear, like a splash of cold water in my face. One minute she was beating the shit out of me, hating me for stealing her husband, and the next she was asking me to get her off. She placed her hands on either side of my face and guided me down between her thighs. She smelled like Kenyatta. Not like she'd had sex with him, but like she was him. They smelled exactly the same. When I sucked her engorged clitoris between my lips and flicked it with my tongue, it was easy to imagine that I was pleasuring Kenyatta. I imagined I was sucking his cock as I swirled my tongue around the little nub and heard Angela's deep-throated moans. Her legs quivered and her long manicured nails snarled in my hair, pulling me deeper, grinding her sex into my face.

"Oh, shit! Oh. Shit! Lick this pussy, bitch! Damn, that feels good."

I didn't know what was happening, what this meant. I wasn't sure if this was meant to be another humiliation or if Angela was really into chicks, if she was into me. I slid my tongue up inside her, straining to find her G-spot with the tip of my tongue. Angela pulled my face hard against her sex until she was practically smothering me. I went back to sucking and licking her clitoris, replacing my tongue with my fingers. I fucked her with two fingers as I flicked my tongue across her engorged nub. Angela's legs shook as the first orgasm struck.

"Oh, my God! Oh, shit! Oh, fuck!"

I lifted her legs up onto my shoulders and licked even faster, then I did something Kenyatta had done to me many times, but that I'd never done to anyone before. I licked my way down past her vagina to her perineum. I licked the small flap of flesh there eliciting even louder moans from Angela then I went lower, easing my tongue into her rectum, flicking it in and out. Angela went wild. This time she screamed when she came.

When it was over, Angela sat staring at me. The expression on her face was no longer one of anger, but simple curiosity. I wondered how this fit into Kenyatta's plan. I wondered if his book had described a scenario like this between the mistress of the house and the house slave. I wondered what Kenyatta would say when he found out. Had I broken some rule? I didn't know.

Angela shook her head then reached out and rubbed a hand over my breasts. Then down between my thighs. She was still rubbing my tits when she began talking to me. She slid down from the chair onto the floor with me.

"Kenyatta and I didn't break up because of you. Not just because of you anyway. We broke up because, after countless threesomes with dozens of different women, I realized that I preferred the women to him. I realized I wasn't bisexual. I was a lesbian."

I was shocked. Did Kenyatta know? What the fuck did this have to do with the oppression of black folks?

"I'm sure this sort of thing happened all the time back in the days of slavery. A lesbian had to be careful in those times. She couldn't just go to the local dyke bar and pick up a chick, but here were these beautiful helpless slaves who had to do whatever she said. You think they didn't take advantage? Gay men too."

Of course it made sense, but I knew she was just rationalizing her own exploitation of the situation between Kenyatta and I and now the three of us. Shit had just gotten a hell of a lot more complicated.

"What do I say to Kenyatta?"

Angela shrugged.

"Tell him whatever you want. I don't care what that nigga thinks."

She laughed at the shocked expression on my face.

"Oh, does that word offend you? Nigga? You sayin' you've never said it?"

I shook my head.

"Bullshit," she said. "And if you haven't said it, you've damn sure thought it. The difference is I'm allowed to say it. You ain't. I don't care what Kenyatta puts you through, you ain't never gonna be down enough to use that word. You ain't never gonna earn the right to use it. Because at any time you can just say fuck this and go back to your little privileged lily white world. Ain't none of this shit real. You're just pretending. See we didn't choose this shit like you did. Nobody gave us a choice or a safe word we could use to escape anytime we wanted. This is real for us."

The mean, hateful Angela was back. The taste of her pussy was still lying heavy on my tongue. She still had one of my breasts in her hands and she was already back to talking shit.

"What have you gone through to give you the right? You were never a slave. You were never oppressed," I said before I could stop myself. Angela's caressing hands became vises, clamping down and twisting my breasts until I squealed and pleaded with her.

"Ouch! Ouch! Stop!"

"I haven't suffered? I haven't suffered? Bitch, what the fuck you know about me?"

As always, I had said the wrong thing, but this wasn't Kenyatta, always the master of his emotions, this was an unstable dyke with a bullwhip I had just pissed off.

"I don't... I-I don't know anything about you."

"Damn right you don't know shit about me. I've been struggling and suffering since the day I was born because of the color of my skin. Looked down upon by stuck-up white bitches like you, followed around department stores by security, passed over for promotions, passed over by all the good black men who would rather chase white pussy!"

I wanted to point out the obvious fact that she was clearly gay and ask her what difference it made since she wasn't interested in men anymore anyway. I wanted to tell her that no man was promised to any woman. That it wasn't like she had put her application in and been passed over in favor of the less qualified white applicant like some kind of reverse affirmative action. All men were up for grabs, regardless of race. Instead, I stayed quiet.

"Get the fuck back out in the yard. Get out of my sight, you stupid bitch!"

She stood up and began kicking me in my ribs and arms, before landing her heel square in my ass as I scrambled out the door to my little shack in the backyard. I wasn't tired, physically, but mentally I felt like I'd just run a marathon wearing a fifty-pound backpack. I was so confused, so aggravated, angry, sad, excited, aroused, and lost, completely and utterly adrift. My entire world had been stripped away from me. The ground had dropped out from beneath my feet and left me floating in space with Kenyatta as my only anchor to earth, but he wasn't here and the bitch who used to be his wife was. I knew Kenyatta would make it all better when he got home. He had to, because I didn't know if I could take this shit much longer.

CHAPTER VI

The night was cool, damp. The fog rolled in and swallowed the stars. The darkness was total. I had a panicked moment, imagining myself back in the box, in that dank, humid basement, but the chill breeze drafting through the cracks in the rickety shack I now called home, reminded me where I was. I pulled the scratchy wool blanket tight around me, shivering. Miserable. I wondered what time Kenyatta would be home, if he would come to the shack or spend the evening with Angela. Being his slave was one thing, but sitting in an old tool shed, shivering in the dark on my bed of straw while he fucked his ex-wife on sheets I helped him pick out, was too much.

The mating calls of cicadas chirped all around, a choir of amorous insects singing out in the darkness. Lights from the houses on either side of the yard cast a faint glow, creating ominous shadows that flickered across the lawn, the fence, and the walls of the shed. I watched them, expecting at any moment that one of the shadows would be Kenyatta coming to rescue me from this misery, take me in his arms, upstairs into his bed. But there was also the fear that a stranger might take

advantage of my helplessness. A neighbor who'd seen
me come out in the yard by myself. A burglar coming to
rob the house. Some random pervert walking by.

My breath quickened and I looked around the shed
for something to defend myself with should it come to
that. I seized a branch that lay in the dirt by my bed of
straw and cradled it against my breasts. I closed my
eyes, trying to sleep. My body was exhausted. The welts
on my back sang out in pain and I was still shivering.
Eventually, the exhaustion won out and I fell into a
dreamless sleep.

The sunlight speared through my eyelids. My joints
ached and the numerous welts, cuts, and bruises
reminded me of their presence with renewed agony. I
had slept straight through to morning and Kenyatta had
not come to visit me. I squinted, shielding my eyes from
the light. It was time to cook breakfast.

There was a hose in the backyard. That would have
to suffice for a shower. I wondered if I could make it
stretch over to the shed where I might at least be able to
use the drafty old structure to shield my body from the
view of curious neighbors. I had no change of clothes,
so I would have to put the same filthy rags I'd worn the
previous day back on.

I turned on the outside faucet and dragged the hose
over to the shed and stripped down. The shirt stuck to
my back and pulling it off ripped a few scabs reopening
the wounds. Blood dripped down my back, and I
dreaded the feel of the water on the freshly bleeding
wounds as much as I welcomed the notion of being
clean again. I held the hose above my head and let the

water pour down over my naked body. I closed my eyes and forgot about everything but the cool water. Even the pain of my welts and cuts didn't bother me. When I opened my eyes, Kenyatta was standing there, impeccably dressed as always, in a dark suit and a black turtleneck. It was a different suit than the one he'd worn to the slave auction, but the look and the effect were the same. I couldn't help but think the choice was deliberate.

"You're late. Breakfast should have been on the table an hour ago. Your mistress is upset with you and so am I. She thinks you should be punished. What do you think?"

I dropped the hose in the grass and stood there, naked and shivering, not knowing what to say. Kenyatta's eyes roved my naked flesh and I looked down at his crotch to see if he liked what he saw. Apparently he did. There was a noticeable bulge in his pants. I walked over to him and took his hardening flesh in hand, stroking him through his pants.

"I am sorry. Let me make it up to you."

I led him into the shed, hoping that bitch was watching. Let her make her own fucking breakfast. The shed door slammed behind us and Kenyatta's hands were all over me, squeezing my breasts, rolling my swollen nipples between his fingers. He kissed the nape of my neck, down between my shoulder blades, to the small of my back. I felt his hot breath against the cleft of my buttocks and then his lips, gently kissing each cheek, his tongue flickering up the crack of my ass before sliding deep inside me. His hand reached up between my legs and his fingers found my clitoris, rubbing it as he fucked my anus with his tongue. I came so quickly, so suddenly, I barely had time to enjoy it. My legs weakened and I almost collapsed. Then Kenyatta was behind me, unbuckling his belt and unzipping his pants. I felt that first passionate invasion. My handsome lover, my Master, thrusting his tumescent flesh inside me. I cried out as his length filled me, hard, throbbing. His breath heavy on the back of my neck.

"Cum inside me. I want to have your babies. I want to be yours forever."

"Yes!" he replied as he sped up his rhythm, thrusting harder, deeper, faster. His fingers dug into the flesh of my hips, rocking me back against him.

"Cum inside me! I want your seed inside me, Master! I want to carry your children!"

I didn't know if I was making him angry, but I was telling the truth. I wanted his children inside me. I wanted to be the mother of his heirs. His thrusts became more urgent, more aggressive and it was difficult to tell if his increased passion was anger or rapture. He turned me around, laid me on my back, and slid himself inside me again. Face to face now, I repeated my declaration.

"I love you, Kenyatta. I want to be the mother of your children. Do you love me?"

He thrust harder, pounding me into the ground.

"Do you love me? Do you want to cum inside me, Master? Do you want me to carry your children?"

"Yes!"

I didn't know which one he was replying to. I knew he loved me, but did he want me to raise his children?

I'd heard him say once, that whenever he found himself falling too hard for a woman, he would imagine her raising his children and that usually sobered him up.

"A woman might be fun to kick it with, party with, have sex with, but that doesn't mean you want her raising your kids. Just because she's a good fuck doesn't mean she'd be a good mom," he'd once said.

I wondered if that's how he thought about me, but asking him now would kill the mood and I wanted to feel him cum inside me. I needed it. It was ridiculous, but I felt like it would somehow validate his love for me. It would take something away from the evil bitch who was sleeping in my bed right now.

Kenyatta's eyes bore into mine. His expression was intense, concentrated. I kissed him and he pressed his lips hard against mine, bruising them in his passion. His tongue darted into my mouth, and I sucked it the way I'd sucked his cock so often. When he pulled his lips away, I whispered to him.

"I love you."

And I could see his eyes soften. Then his head whipped back, his body stiffened, and he let out a roar. I grabbed his hard buttocks and pulled him deeper, held him there as he orgasmed. Imagining his seed spilling inside me sparked my own climax and soon my cries of ecstasy joined his guttural moans. He collapsed on top of me and I held him there, keeping him inside me, not wanting him to leave, ever. I wanted to die there with him on top of me, inside of me. I would have been perfectly satisfied and content to expire in the arms of the man I loved. That would have meant an end to my trials. But it wasn't to be.

Kenyatta stood, pulled up his pants, zipped them, and buckled his belt. He buttoned his suit jacket and smoothed the lapels.

"Your Mistress is awake. Make sure she has breakfast. Don't be late again. When the sun rises, you rise."

He turned and walked out of my little shack, leaving me desperately confused and frustrated. I rose to my feet and took a deep breath, preparing myself to confront that hateful bitch again. I smoothed out the wrinkles in my simple frock, slid my feet into a pair of slippers that had been left for me, and walked into the house. Angela was waiting.

"What the fuck took you so long? I want coffee and eggs, now! You want another whipping like yesterday? Does that turn your freaky ass on or something? Is that why Kenyatta likes your stank ass? Because both of you motherfuckers are perverts?"

"I don't know, ma'am."

She was sitting at the table again, wearing the same terry cloth robe, naked underneath, slightly open, revealing that flawless athletic physique. I tried not to stare at her and went about making her coffee and cooking her eggs.

"You're cleaning this entire house today. I want you to scrub the floors, the walls, the baseboards, dust all the lamps, and the ceiling fans, every-fucking-thing. You hear?"

"Yes, ma'am."

I turned on one of the burners, pulled out a large Teflon skillet, and cracked two eggs onto it.

"Sunny side up!"

"Yes, ma'am."

I was going to "yes, ma'am" this bitch to death. I refused to be broken. After finishing her eggs, I lifted them onto a plate with a spatula, careful not to break the yolks. I brought the plate and the coffee to Angela. Then turned to begin cleaning the kitchen.

"Uh uh. You stand right here until I'm done eating. And strip. I want to look at you."

"Yes, ma'am."

As commanded, I removed my dress and then my bra and underwear. I stood in front of the kitchen table with my arms at my sides, feeling self-conscious and slightly ridiculous.

"You are a sexy bitch, ain't you? I'll give that nigga credit. He does know how to pick 'em. You think you look as good as me, bitch?" Angela said, wiping her mouth with a napkin after swallowing another fork full of eggs, then rising and letting her robe slip to the floor.

"No, ma'am."

"Look at me, bitch! You think I'm sexy?"

I let my eyes rove over her nude form, her muscular arms and shoulders, flat stomach with sculpted abs, small perky breasts, muscular thighs, tight little ass.

"Yes, ma'am."

"Yes, ma'am, what?"

"Yes, ma'am. I think you're sexy."

"You want to lick this pussy again?" she said, running her fingers up her thighs and then between them, winding her hips like she was dancing to a slow reggae rhythm. She was one fine piece of ass. It did make me wonder again what Kenyatta saw in me when he could have been fucking Angela every night. Even if she was a closet lesbian. Then I wondered if he was fucking her every night. I wanted to ask her but feared her response.

"Say it! Say you want to lick this pussy."

I had no choice. As long as I was part of this experiment, she was in control. Disobeying her would mean losing Kenyatta. I wondered if Kenyatta even knew the things Angela was making me do.

"I want to lick your pussy," I said in a monotone voice, staring at a spot just over Angela's shoulder, avoiding eye contact. She didn't seem to care. A complicit, enthusiastic partner wasn't what she was after. She wanted to humiliate and debase me. My eager consent would have ruined the thrill.

"Get on your knees, white bitch," she said with a smile.

I knelt on the floor in front of Angela, and she walked over and placed one leg on the table, opening her thighs and giving me an unobstructed view of her neatly shaven vagina. She grabbed me by the back of the head and thrust my face into her sex. Wanting it to be over as soon as possible, I sucked and licked at her clitoris, aggressively, driving her toward orgasm at a hundred miles an hour.

"Slow down!" she said, but I could already feel the trembling in her legs, see her stomach tighten, hear her breath quicken and deepen, taste the juices flowing from her labia. She was close. I flicked my tongue across her clit rapidly, battering it like a speed bag until I felt her nails dig into my scalp and a moan catch in her throat, low and sultry before becoming a scream of purest ecstasy. As long as I could do this to her, I owned this bitch, more than she could ever own me.

She collapsed against the kitchen table, spilling her coffee and almost knocking her plate onto the floor. I quickly rose, snatched up a rag, and began cleaning up the mess. I could feel Angela's eyes on me.

"You hate me don't you?"

I didn't reply. I finished wiping up her coffee and removed her plate, rinsing it off in the sink and placing it in the dishwasher. I could still feel Angela's eyes drilling into me. I poured her another cup of coffee and handed it to her. Her eyes narrowed, nostrils flared, and a scowl snarled her lips. Angela shook her head as she took the coffee from me. She took a sip then regarded me with the most curious expression. Clearly, I was some sort of enigma to her and her inability to pigeonhole me frustrated her.

"I'm not the one you should be hating," she said. "You think Kenyatta doesn't know about all of this? You think he didn't know exactly what he was doing when he brought me in here? You are a stupid bitch. You'll see. You'll see."

She closed her robe and walked out of the room.

I spent the rest of the day doing exactly as Angela had commanded. I scrubbed the floors, did the laundry, wiped down the walls, dusted all the appliances and light fixtures, cleaned the toilets and tubs, then made her lunch: ham and cheese on rye, and a spinach salad with sliced apples, cranberries, red onions, blue cheese, and balsamic vinaigrette. I served her in the dining room, so I would be far away from her while she ate. I wanted to avoid a repeat of this morning.

In the kitchen, I made my own salad and ate quickly, making sure I was done before Angela was, so I could clear her dishes. She glared at me as I whisked in and out of the room. Occasionally, she treated me to more of her insights into my relationship with Kenyatta.

"You must enjoy being used like a piece of trash."

"I'm telling you, Kenyatta's going to wipe his ass with you and toss you aside. He ain't never marrying you, girl. You'd be better off sticking with them white boys. You know niggas ain't shit. The only reason a guy like Kenyatta is interested in you is because he can do whatever he wants to you and you'll put up with it. He knows he can't treat no sister like this."

It took great effort to hold my tongue. Obviously, the fact that if he was using me then he was using her too, had not yet occurred to her. He had brought her into this house to help prepare her successor, to spend every day with the woman he was fucking, the woman he was fucking even while Angela was right there in the house. It had to hurt. I could see her pain every time she tried to convince me to leave, every time she tried to break me, even while she was punishing me or using me for sex. The fact that Kenyatta had chosen another woman, a white woman, was an open sore on Angela's heart.

I was in the kitchen, cooking dinner, when Kenyatta came home. Immediately, I could tell that something was wrong. He smiled at me as he rushed past me, pulled a beer from the refrigerator, then took it with him to the bedroom. I wanted so bad to ask him what was troubling him. Normally, I would have, but I didn't dare with Angela there.

There was a baked chicken in the oven and mashed potatoes and corn on the cob on the stove. I worried for a moment that it would go to waste. Regardless of my worries, I continued preparing the meal. I set the dining room table, folded the napkins and laid out the silverware and plates. I stopped short of lighting a candle. There was no way I was going to prepare a romantic dinner for my man and his ex-wife.

It felt weird to think of Kenyatta as "my man," but I felt more connected to him since the experiment began than I had at any other time in our relationship. I wasn't sure what that meant for our relationship. For weeks now, he had been my Master. It was already getting hard to remember when I wasn't his property, when I wasn't a slave. I wondered how successful we would be at resuming our normal roles when the time came. If the time came.

Kenyatta came back downstairs wearing a robe and black and white checkered pajama pants. He sat down at the table and stared straight ahead, avoiding eye contact with both Angela and I. He barely seemed to notice we were in the same room. Angela sat down at the table across from Kenyatta, but didn't attempt to speak to him. She fidgeted nervously in her chair, rearranging the silverware and trying to catch Kenyatta's eye. Whatever he was thinking, Angela didn't know any more about it than I did, and it was clear that she couldn't handle being in the dark.

He finished his meal, and I quickly cleared the table. When he looked at me, there was a sadness in his eyes that ratcheted up my anxiety to nerve-rattling levels. Was he about to tell me this was all a big mistake? That the experiment was over and he was going back to Angela? I wanted to ask him what he was thinking so badly it was killing me.

He turned to Angela with that baleful expression and told her to go upstairs.

"Why?"

"Because I said so."

"So you can fuck this slave in our house?"

"MY house and I'll do whatever the hell I want in my house. You're a guest here. Now go upstairs!"

Chastened, and clearly frightened of him, Angela left the room, casting one last hateful glance my way that promised retribution. I had never seen Kenyatta so forceful with her before, had never imagined that she would have stood for such a thing. I guess I believed the stereotype about black women not taking shit from anyone. Seeing Kenyatta dismiss her so bluntly was revelatory. I knew Angela would make me suffer for it, but I was far more worried about whatever was plaguing Kenyatta's thoughts.

"Come here, Kitten."

It felt like ages had passed since he'd called me kitten. Not since the night of the slave auction. My heart melted at the words, but somehow, hearing such endearing words come from his mouth deepened my fear. Why was he being so nice to me unless he were trying to soften a blow? I only hoped the blow would be physical.

"Yes, Master?"

Kenyatta smiled.

"Be my kitten tonight."

I knew what he meant. I stripped quickly, tossing my clothes aside and dropping down on all fours. I purred as I rubbed my face against his pant leg and curled up at his feet. He patted his thigh and I climbed up into his lap, nuzzling my face in his neck as I continued to purr. I lightly clawed his back through his shirt. Kenyatta ran his hand from the top of my head to the small of my back, petting me as he held me in his lap. His eyes remained fixed on some distant thought, gazing across the room at the bare wall.

He held me like that for nearly an hour, before patting me on my head and sending me back into the kitchen to finish cleaning. I crawled in on my hands and knees, knowing how much it usually turned him on to see me crawl naked across the floor. His eyes followed me and I could see the lust in them, but it was almost obscured by the anxiety still clouding his expression. Something was definitely wrong with him. He was still watching me as I began washing the dishes. I was still unclothed, and usually watching me do chores naked would have been irresistible to him, but not tonight. When I turned back to look at him, after placing the last dish in the dishwasher, he had already left the room. Still confused and deeply concerned, I gathered my clothes and walked back out to my shack.

CHAPTER VII

I was awakened by the morning sun beaming through the wooden slats of my shed. A sparkling white and yellow brilliance invaded my eyelids and my dreams, wrenching me from fantasies of domestic bliss back into my little backyard hell.

I had barely slept and felt exhausted. The previous night's anxiety weighed on me. I could not stop thinking about Kenyatta, wondering what awful news was troubling him that would soon be troubling me. After quickly hosing myself off, I threw on my old rags and rushed into the kitchen to get breakfast ready.

Above me, I could hear Kenyatta and Angela arguing, but I couldn't hear well enough to get what they were arguing about. I heard my name several times followed by exclamations like "Fuck that bitch!" and "Who cares where she goes!" That last one scared me most of all. *Who cares where she goes?* Where was I going? Was Kenyatta sending me away? Because of that bitch?

The argument ended, and I heard the shower turn on. I also heard the sound of footsteps descending the stairs. I wiped an unexpected tear from my eyes and tried to stop the trembling in my lips as I flipped pancakes and fried bacon. Angela sat down at the table with a smug expression on her face. At first I assumed it meant she had won the argument, then I noticed the pain in the creases of her smile, the jealous gleam in her eye, and I knew that, whatever she had wanted Kenyatta to do to me, she hadn't gotten her way. There was so much naked hate in her expression that I couldn't stand to look at her and kept my eyes averted.

Kenyatta came down next wearing a dark blue, pinstriped suit with a light blue shirt and a red tie. He looked like a politician. It almost made me laugh. Still, he looked damn good.

He kissed me on the cheek and playfully swatted my ass before sitting down at the table across from Angela. She was livid. I got the clear impression that she wanted to murder me in front of him, right there in the kitchen. I handed her a cup of coffee and braced for her to throw it in my face. A warning glare from Kenyatta was the only thing that saved me from a horrible scalding. But Kenyatta was leaving in a few minutes and once Angela and I were alone, I knew I was fucked.

Kenyatta kissed Angela on the cheek and said goodbye, then he did the same to me. He paused and brushed the hair from my eyes. I smiled and dropped my gaze to the floor. He placed a finger under my chin and lifted my head so I was looking him directly in the eyes. That familiar flutter returned in the pit of my stomach. He was so handsome.

"Hang in there, Kitten. I'll be home soon."

That same sadness was still in his eyes when they locked with mine. Whatever was bothering him had not yet been resolved. It was also clear that he was as worried about leaving me alone with Angela as I was.

"Take good care of your Mistress today," Kenyatta said. "She got up on the wrong side of the bed this morning."

He kissed me on the forehead, then glared another warning at Angela before grabbing his briefcase and heading out the door. I stared at the closed door like it was the locked door of a tomb or a prison cell. The knots in my stomach twisted tighter when I heard Kenyatta's car start and then pull out of the driveway.

"Come with me."

Angela's voice sent a cold chill through my bones. Whatever she wanted me to come see or do was bound to be painful and/or humiliating. Refusing her, however, was not an option. I followed her tight little ass up the stairs. When she passed the master bedroom, the guest bath, and the guest bedroom, I knew where she was taking me...the playroom. The dungeon.

We built it a year ago, when our "play" began getting more serious. It contained a stockade, a whipping post, a crucifix, a dentist's chair, and our prized possession: a birthing table complete with stirrups and leather restraints. There was nothing in that room I wanted to experience with Angela.

"You have been a bad girl, Natasha. Or should I call you Kitten? Hmmm?"

I refused to take the bait. I kept my head lowered and my hands clasped in front of me in as submissive a posture as I could manage.

There was a "toy chest" on the far side of the room, a table loaded with whips, flails, canes, and paddles of different sizes and description. Some were made of rubber, some wood, and some leather. Some were knotted and some had spikes. On a small stainless steel instrument tray by the birthing table, were metal dildos, forceps, clamps, catheters, and a stainless steel speculum.

The speculum had been my idea, as had the birthing table. Since my very first OBGYN appointment at fourteen, I had fantasized about meeting a handsome gynecologist who would seduce me while my legs were in the stirrups and so Kenyatta had agreed to do some role-playing.

"Relax, Miss. This won't take long."

He had snapped the latex gloves as he put them on one at a time. Then he squirted lubricant in his hand and eased a finger up inside me. I gasped and clenched, locking down on his finger with my Kegel muscles.

"Relaaaaax," he repeated in that deep sultry voice of his. He began rubbing my clit with his thumb as he eased another finger inside me then another and finally another until he was practically fisting me. Then he eased his thumb inside me as well, while using his other hand to work my clit. I moaned, my legs trembled, as he punched up inside me over and over again. The first orgasm hit me and I thrashed in the restraints. But

Kenyatta wasn't done. He picked up the speculum, lubed it up, and eased it inside me.

He fucked me with it. Thrusting it in and out of me. Then he picked up the metal dildo and used my own juices to lubricate it before easing it into my rectum, while still fucking me with the speculum.

He squeezed the handle, opening me up wide. The cold metal felt uncomfortable and I was almost turned off until I felt Kenyatta's lips and tongue on my clitoris, sucking and licking my body into another violent orgasm.

"Oh God! Oh my fucking, God!"

Kenyatta withdrew the speculum, but left the dildo in my ass as he stood and began to undress. He shrugged out of his lab coat, unbuckled his pants and let them drop to the floor.

"Everything looks perfect down there to me. Let's see how it feels, shall we?"

I nodded my head enthusiastically, practically salivating as he withdrew his massive erection from his pants.

"Yes! Fuck me, Doctor!"

With my legs still strapped in the stirrups, my arms cuffed to the table, and the stainless steel dildo still in my ass like a butt-plug, Kenyatta rammed himself inside me and fucked me hard, gripping the sides of the table and almost lifting it off the floor as he pounded into me.

The memory sent little shocks through my loins. The lab coat still sat on a hook beside the table. I wanted to hold it to my chest, hold it to my nose and inhale, hoping it would still smell like Kenyatta. Whatever

Angela had planned, I knew it would not be nearly as pleasant. I tried to imagine what Angela would do if she had me strapped into those stirrups with scalpels and a speculum at her disposal. I shuddered at the thought.

Luckily, Angela wasn't very creative. I doubt she'd have known what half the instruments were used for or that she'd have had the stomach for it. Instead, she grabbed a knotted cat o' nine tails. As painful as I knew the cat was, at least it was a familiar pain.

"Strip off those clothes!"

I let the dress fall to my feet. I felt Angela's gaze all over me.

"Get over there! Put your hands on that post!"

The whipping post was a thick pillar, seven feet tall and the circumference of a telephone pole. It had two metal loops attached to either side of it, two near the top and two near the bottom, and there was a strip of leather attached to each one. I turned around and held on to the metal ringlets. Angela stepped forward and tied my wrists to the loops.

"I am really beginning to get in to this shit," she whispered in my ear. Her breath smelled like mouthwash and syrup.

I knew she wanted me to beg, whimper, plead with her. It wasn't going to happen. I could take whatever she could give and more. All the shit I'd gone through in my life. Being raped and molested when I was barely in my teens. Being broke, homeless, hungry. Being beaten up by boyfriends, cheated on, lied to, used, and stolen from. There was nothing this bitch could do to break me. Bring it the fuck on!

Angela cracked the cat hard across my back with a loud *whap!* The slapping sound hit simultaneous with the braided leather cutting through my skin and the pain that seemed to slice through the muscle into the bone. The air whooshed out of my lungs. I gritted my teeth to keep from screaming.

Again and again, Angela cracked the cat o' nine tails with all her might, ripping deep grooves in my flesh and turning my back into a bloody mess, painting the walls with my blood. I knew I would keep these wounds for the rest of my life. I closed my eyes and imagined that Kenyatta held the cat instead of his spiteful ex-wife. In a way, he did. Angela was little more than his proxy. Whether she realized it or not, he was swinging the cat vicariously. She was just another tool for my education in the black experience, like the box in the basement or the shed in the backyard or the whipping post. Even when I was licking this bitch's cunt, it was at Kenyatta's behest.

"I love you, Kenyatta," I whispered.

The whip cracked again.

"I love you, Kenyatta," I said louder as the braided leather cut into me again. My legs went weak as the pain began to overcome me.

"I love you, Kenyatta!" I yelled. This time, the cat did not land again.

I heard the cat o' nine tails drop to the floor and then Angela's footsteps walking toward me. She stepped around in front of me. I saw her through a dizzying fog of pure pain. I was panting hard, exhausted. My body shivered with agony. I was on the verge of collapse.

Angela grabbed me by the chin with her long, French-manicured nails. I was in so much pain I couldn't lift my head without assistance.

"I love you, Kenyatta," I whispered.

"Shut-the-fuck-up."

"I love you, Kenyatta," I whispered again.

The blow came suddenly and unexpectedly. Her palm smacked across my cheek with a loud *pop!* like a gunshot. The room spun then came into crisp focus. Angela's furious stare hovered inches from my face.

"You are fucking crazy."

She pulled a leather hood over my head. It had a zipper up the back and a zipper where the eyeholes were. The opening for the mouth was a hard plastic circle. Angela picked up a small, flexible, clear dildo and held it up to the hood's mouth opening, pressing it against my lips.

"Open!"

I opened my mouth and she eased the Jell-O-textured little dildo between my lips and partially into my throat. Just when I felt myself beginning to gag. It stopped. Luckily, it was only six-inches long, and having sucked Kenyatta's cock for months, I was accustomed to at least another two inches.

She walked across the room and picked up a strap-on dildo. This was a new addition, something she'd brought with her. The harness was made of black latex and leather and there was a nine-inch, pink, flexible dildo strapped into it, the father of the one that was currently filling my throat. Angela picked up a small vial of lube and slathered the dildo with it. She closed the mouth-slit, preventing me from spitting out the dildo, then she closed the two eye-slits, leaving me blind, anxious, and a little fearful.

I felt Angela's hands on my breasts, then her lips, sucking my nipples. She took her time, sucking each one hungrily, then she stepped behind me. I felt her hands on my thighs, slowly caressing them. She rubbed my ass, jiggled my corpulent buttocks, smacked each cheek hard then kissed them lovingly. I felt her tongue flick along the crack of my ass before she bit and sucked on my ass cheeks. Then her hands went back to my thighs, slowly parting my legs.

Her body pressed against mine. Her breath was hot and moist on the back of my neck and her hands soft but brutal as they found my breasts again, squeezing them, tweaking the nipples. She whispered huskily in my ear, voice heavy with lust.

"I'm going to fuck the shit out of you."

Her lubed fingers slid between my legs, up inside me. They were cool and slippery from the lubricant. She parted my labia and pressed her hips against my ass as she eased the dildo into my pussy. I gasped as the stiff, jelly-like phallus filled me and Angela began thrusting aggressively. She moaned in my ear, as if it were her own flesh inside me rather than rubber.

She untied me and I collapsed. Angela stormed out of the room and left me trembling on the floor. I could feel my sanity beginning to slip, but I thought of Kenyatta and I held on. I held on to the image of us as a family raising kids together. It was my lifeline in this sea of madness.

CHAPTER VIII

Kenyatta became increasingly affectionate toward me over the following weeks. When he saw the damage Angela had done to me, he threatened to kick her out of the house if it ever happened again. For her part, Angela never used the whip again, switching to paddles and canes and making sure to use them on my ass and thighs, which had regained much of their former weight now that I was eating table scraps instead of horse beans and yams. I would have never admitted it to her, but I was actually beginning to enjoy the spankings.

I was vacuuming the living room while, in the next room, Angela was working out that flawless body of hers. I could hear her doing squats and lunges with a pair of Kenyatta's huge dumbbells. Her workout routine would have put half the men I knew to shame. She could bench press a hundred pounds, squat two hundred pounds, and curl seventy-five pounds. There was a heavy bag in there as well and, after finishing her last set of lunges, she pulled on a pair of gloves and began throwing combinations, grunting with each blow. If it ever came down to it, as tiny as she was, I didn't think I could take her. Each time her fists pounded the bag, I winced, imagining those same fists crashing into my body.

I was almost finished cleaning the living room when Angela walked in wearing tight black yoga pants and a pink halter top that came to just beneath her breasts and accentuated her incredible abdominal muscles. She sat down on Kenyatta's lounge chair, still breathing hard, wiping sweat from her brow with a towel. She had a paddle in her hands. I didn't need to wait to be told. I dropped my dress and underwear, walked over to her and laid across her thighs.

Angela smiled. "I think you're starting to like this," she purred, rubbing my naked ass. She reached a hand between my legs. I was already moist. I gasped as she slid a finger up inside me, withdrew it, then licked my juices from her fingertip. "Mmmm. You do like this don't you?"

She smacked my ass hard with her bare hand. "Don't you?"

"Yes, Mistress. I like it."

She rubbed my bare ass where she had just smacked it and I squirmed, waiting for the next blow.

"Maybe I can help you enjoy it a little more."

Angela parted my thighs and began rubbing my clitoris. I moaned, closed my eyes, and once again imagined that it was Kenyatta's hands between my thighs. Then she brought the paddle down hard against my ass.

"Oh!"

"You like it?"

She was flicking her fingertips across my clitoris, rubbing it, twirling her index finger around the swollen nub. I moaned louder, my thighs quivered and I squirmed in her lap.

"Yes, Mistress. I love it!"

She brought down the paddle again, harder this time, sending a shock through my thighs and bringing me closer to orgasm. Kenyatta had done a wonderful job teaching me to enjoy the pain. What Angela was doing now, was almost identical to the first time he'd paddled me. I was certain she had learned the technique from him. I felt a twinge of jealousy imagining Angela bent over Kenyatta's knee being paddled and finger-fucked. But Angela's fingers were so talented, I soon lost myself in waves of luxurious pleasure. This bitch knew her way around some pussy.

I was on the verge of orgasm when Angela flipped me over, lying me on the couch with my legs in the air and burying her face between them. She sucked and licked my clitoris aggressively, angrily, wrapping her powerful arms around my thighs and holding me in place, wrestling me toward climax.

A roller coaster of orgasms barreled through me at a hundred miles an hour. I screamed and clawed the couch cushions. When Angela lifted her head from between my thighs, licking my juices from her full, heart-shaped lips, there was a triumphant smile on her face. I knew the feeling. Making someone cum was power. It was the only power I had over Angela and she had just taken it back. But there was a difference, I still had Kenyatta.

She slid her hands over my body, up my stomach, and over my breasts, which had also regained most of their former size. They filled her hands, she tweaked each nipple, rolling them between her fingers.

"Your breasts are wonderful," Angela said. She crawled up my body and sucked one of my nipples into her mouth. I sighed deeply, grabbing the back of her head and holding it against my chest while her tongue swirled around my nipple. Slowly, she kissed her way back down my body. I opened my eyes when I felt her tongue slide up inside me. That's when I saw Kenyatta standing above us.

"Oh, shit!"

I scrambled away from Angela. She looked up, and when she spotted Kenyatta, the fear in her eyes was genuine and profound. I wondered what Kenyatta had done to her to make Angela so terrified of him.

"It's great to see you two getting along so well," he said, sneering in disgust. "Don't stop just because I'm here. Keep going."

"I-I'm sorry, Kenyatta. I didn't mean to…" Angela stammered.

"I said, keep going. I believe you were licking my slave's pussy. So, lick her pussy. Do it! Now!"

He grabbed Angela by the back of the head and forced it back down between my thighs.

"How often do you think the lady of the house licked her slave's pussy? You are way off script, Angela. Are you trying to fuck this whole thing up? You trying to sabotage my shit?"

"No! I wouldn't do that, Kenyatta! I swear! I was just...there were lesbians back then too and some of them had slaves. I bet this type of shit happened all the time."

Kenyatta pushed her head back between my thighs, crushing her mouth into my sex. I could feel her lips trembling against my clitoris.

"I told you to keep licking!" Kenyatta bellowed. There was madness in his eyes. A chill of fear went through me as well. I didn't know what he was going to do to us.

"And you! I've got something else for you to do."

Kenyatta stripped out of his suit. He folded his sports coat, pants, shirt, and tie, and draped them carefully over the back of his lounge chair. Then he pulled off his pants and I was more than a little relieved to see that his cock was hard. If he was aroused, then he wasn't that angry with me.

He walked over to the couch, his stiff cock bobbing in the air in front of him. Angela had begun ferociously licking, sucking, and even biting at my swollen labia. My fear gave way to pleasure as Angela's talented tongue brutally lashed my engorged clitoris. I watched Kenyatta's throbbing hard erection jab at my face and I opened my mouth to receive him. He was not gentle, as he thrust his cock between my lips and began raping my throat. His hard fingers gripped the back of my head and he thrust his hips forward, fucking my throat. I could feel his erection slide past my tonsils and I fought hard to stifle my gag reflex. Tears wept from my eyes as I struggled to keep from regurgitating all over Kenyatta's magnificent penis.

Kenyatta eased his cock out of my throat, walked to the end of the couch, behind Angela, and ripped her shorts down.

"No! No, Kenyatta, don't!" I begged. Angela glanced up from between my legs and there was an unfamiliar look in her eyes, sympathy. Then she grimaced as Kenyatta eased his cock inside her and began pounding her vagina while she continued sucking my clit and tears spilled down my cheeks. Kenyatta locked eyes with me. His eyes were ferocious. He was angry, but he was enjoying himself, enjoying my pain. Angela's grunts and groans filled my ears and I screamed to drown them out.

We switched places. Kenyatta pulled out of Angela, flipped her over, then bent me over so my face was between her legs and hers between mine, then he smacked my ass several times while Angela fluttered her tongue across my clit like hummingbird wings. When he gripped my hips in his powerful hands and slammed his cock inside of me, the feel of Angela's tongue on my clit and Kenyatta's enormous cock thrusting deep inside me, brought me to a climax so powerful it felt like every muscle in my body was spasming at once. The pleasure was so overwhelming I didn't think I could stand it. I collapsed on Angela's face and she continued sucking my clit, bringing me to another orgasm and another and another. I lowered my head and stabbed my tongue into the sopping wetness between Angela's thighs, returning the favor, licking her swollen clit until she screamed her pleasure at the top of her lungs.

Kenyatta withdrew his cock and ordered us both on to our knees. He slid his throbbing erection between my breasts, fucking my cleavage while Angela licked the head of his cock. My jealousy was gone now, incinerated in the first explosive orgasm. They were both my lovers now. I wanted to please them both, equally. When Angela began sucking Kenyatta's cock, gagging and choking on it as she took his full length down her throat, I didn't hesitate. I leaned down and began sucking and licking his balls.

His toes curled. His muscular thighs quivered. I knew he was about to cum. I stopped licking his balls and sat up straight, lifting my breasts so he could ejaculate on them. Angela stopped sucking his cock just as he was about to explode and began licking my nipples. Kenyatta ejaculated on my breasts and Angela's lips and tongue simultaneously, and Angela licked it up, every drop, lapping the cum from my nipples and cleavage, the tip of his penis, and her own lips. It had been amazing, but I wasn't sure what it meant for the game, the experiment. This wasn't how it was supposed to go. Was the game ruined now? Was it over? I didn't know and that made me nervous.

Kenyatta left us both on the floor and began to dress. I opened my mouth to speak, but Angela put a finger to my lips and shook her head. I had to admit that she knew him better than me, so I took her advice and kept my mouth closed.

"Have dinner ready when I get back."

"You're leaving?" Angela said.

Kenyatta scowled down at us and shook his head.

"I have to go back to work. I have clients to see. I only came home because I knew what you bitches were up to. We'll talk about this when I get home."

He traced a line with his finger from Angela to me to the couch when he said "This." Then he turned and walked out the door, leaving Angela and I with a hundred questions, which was exactly what he had intended. He wanted us to drive ourselves crazy wondering what he was planning to do. I hoped he would let this threesome continue, but I couldn't imagine whatever he was thinking of doing would be anything so pleasant.

"I'm sorry, Natasha. I really didn't mean to fuck things up for you. I sorta like you. Really. Even if you are fucking my husband. I hope I didn't ruin everything. I guess I kinda took advantage of the situation a bit."

I didn't say anything. I didn't know what to say. All I could do was hope and pray Kenyatta would give me another chance.

CHAPTER IX

Angela and I worked in the kitchen together, cooking all of Kenyatta's favorites. I seasoned a brisket and slow-cooked it in the oven on 300 degrees, while Angela made wasabi mashed potatoes and broccoli with garlic and butter. Then I threw a bunch of crab legs in a pot to boil. We were both dressed provocatively in corsets, silk panties, garters, and fishnet stockings. We had decided to try to reach Kenyatta through his stomach and his libido.

When Kenyatta walked in, he took one look at us and shook his head. Not to be deterred I dropped to my knees and began unbuttoning his pants.

"Let your kitten relax you, Master."

Angela dropped down beside me and we both pulled out his cock and began licking it up and down. It was working, I could see the steely-eyed resolve in Kenyatta's eyes begin to melt.

"I've made up my mind."

The words hung in the air like a thundercloud. I tried to ignore them and concentrate on sucking his cock, but tears had already begun to well in my eyes.

Angela didn't stop. She was jacking him off while still licking the head of his cock.

"What do you think would happen to a slave if the master came home and found her fucking his wife?" Kenyatta said and I began to shiver. I knew. I knew what he was going to say before he even said it.

"He would whip her," Angela said, still stroking Kenyatta's throbbing erection. "He would whip them both."

"And then?" Kenyatta said, glaring down at us.

"He would kill her? You can't kill her, Kenyatta!"

"Don't be silly! Slaves were expensive. You don't destroy an expensive piece of property unless you don't have any other choice."

"He would sell her," I spoke up. "If a master caught his slave in a lesbian act with his wife, if he didn't kill her, he would sell her away."

Kenyatta nodded and the tears began to flow from my eyes in a torrent.

"No," Angela gasped. "I thought you said you wouldn't sell her?"

"I told you the experiment wouldn't be real if I didn't. This just confirms it."

He had been planning it all along. He was going to sell me to someone else, a new Master. I felt my heart tear slowly. I became lightheaded and almost passed out.

"Please, Master! Please don't sell me! Whip me! Whip me to death, but don't sell me!"

"It's already done. Mistress Delia is coming to collect you in the morning."

I wailed and threw myself at his feet.

"No! No, Master! Pleeeeeease!"

"Like I said, it's already done. It has to be done."

He pulled his now flaccid cock out of Angela's grasp and tucked it back in his pants then he reached down and picked up a book, the book that had started all of this, a book I had come to dread, *400 Years of Oppression*. I didn't want to hear what he had to say.

"No. No. No." I was talking about the book as much as the idea of being sold to that huge leather dyke from the Society of "O." At least it was a woman. The idea of Kenyatta selling me to another man would have been too much for me to take.

"Rebellious slaves were often separated from their families and sold away to other plantations. Often leaving a benevolent owner for a more stern and often crueler master. Some slaves came to love their masters and when they were sold away, were traumatized by both the loss of family and friends and the loss of their beloved masters and the plantations they had considered their home. The wives of slave-owners, who fathered children with slaves, were often the instigators who demanded the owner's slave mistresses be sold away, leaving their children behind."

I wanted to tell him I didn't care anymore. I didn't care about slaves who were sold away from their families, as long as I wasn't sold, as long as I didn't have to suffer the loss of my Master. I didn't want to leave, but I knew it wouldn't matter. There was nothing I could say to change his mind except the safe word that I could never utter.

"Master?"

"Yes?"

"Would you make love to me one last time?"

Angela and I were both still on our knees. Kenyatta's mouth opened to speak, appeared to change his mind, closed his mouth and nodded. Angela hugged me, then stood up. She kissed Kenyatta on the cheek as she walked out of the room.

"Use the bedroom. You two need to be alone. I'm gonna watch some TV."

I cried in Kenyatta's arms that night. We made love slowly, lovingly. I whispered my love to him as I gasped with pleasure, crushed into the mattress beneath his heavily muscled body. His voice was tight, hoarse, when he croaked out a reply.

"I love you too, Kitten."

I couldn't see his eyes in the dark bedroom, even with the moonlight streaming through the open blinds, but I suspected he was crying too.

CHAPTER X

Mistress Delia's breasts were larger than my head. That was my first thought when I saw her walking up to the front door with those titanic mammaries squeezed into a corset that pushed them up beneath her chin like two pale melons. She looked soft and doughy. Her arm fat flapped like wings as she walked and her thighs, easily the circumference of my entire waist, rubbed together from the crotch to just above the knee. Her ass made mine look positively petite. It was the size of a pumpkin—two pumpkins—pressed together and squeezed into a red latex skirt. Her belly stuck out almost as far as her breasts. Everything on her body jiggled when she walked. Next to her, I looked practically emaciated.

I couldn't help wondering if this was how Kenyatta saw me. I knew he'd been intimate with the rotund dominatrix. I wasn't sure who had topped who, but I knew they had played before. I didn't know if he had ever actually fucked her, but, for Kenyatta, the whip could be just as intimate as his cock. If he found this huge woman attractive, and he found me attractive, what did that say about me? Did we look the same in his eyes? I knew the stereotype of black men dating fat white chicks. I hated to think we justified that particular prejudice. Her face made all of that irrelevant, however.

She had the most beautiful eyes I'd ever seen, a brilliant emerald green that looked almost reptilian and contrasted with her flaming red hair. Her lips were painted blood red and her smile revealed perfectly straight, sparkling white teeth with long canines that made her look vampiric. That fat bitch was hot. I had to admit it. Still, I didn't want to be her slave. I had only one Master, Kenyatta, but I would do as he said. If he wanted this bitch to own me, then I was hers.

Kenyatta invited her in, took her hand, bowed, and kissed her knuckles.

"Mistress Delia, you are lovelier than ever."

She did the same, doing a little curtsy and kissing his class ring.

"Hello, King. You are still the most fuckable male in the BDSM scene. And your taste in subs is impeccable as ever. I cannot believe you are really parting with this lovely specimen."

Kenyatta leaned in and kissed Mistress Delia on the lips. I saw him slip his tongue into her mouth and her suck it like it was his cock. Jealousy surged within me. My breath caught in my throat until their lips parted. Kenyatta patted her on her more than ample buttocks then squeezed her titanic breasts and kissed her again.

"Don't go getting me all horny, King. I might take it out on your little Kitten."

She swatted me on my ass with one of her meaty paws and gave it a squeeze. I smiled passively. The co-opting of the nickname Kenyatta had given to me, by this stranger. She had no fucking right to call me that as far as I was concerned, but my outrage was useless. It sat in my gut like bad Mexican food, churning, indigestible.

"Don't worry, Kitten. I won't hurt you...too much," Delia said with a wink.

I turned to Kenyatta, eyes brimming with tears, in one last, desperate attempt to save myself. I saw Angela sitting on the couch, rocking forward and back, biting her bottom lip and squeezing her hands between her knees, desperate to intervene but keeping silent. I couldn't count on her for help. For all I knew, this had all been her doing.

Angela smiled at me and mouthed the words "I'm sorry" as Kenyatta placed an old suitcase on the front porch filled with my meager belongings. Kenyatta turned and brushed the hair from my face, blessing me, for what felt like the last time, with that radiant smile of his. I could see the sorrow in his eyes. The worry. He didn't want me to go either. I could tell. So why the fuck was he sending me away? Was it just for the game, so I would experience what his ancestors experienced, or was he jealous of Angela? He couldn't really think I would leave him for that hateful bitch. Even though she licked pussy like she was bred for the act, there was no forgetting the hell she had put me through. I didn't trust her.

"You do what Mistress Delia tells you, okay? You are hers now," Kenyatta said, sounding like he was sending a child off to college rather than giving the woman he claimed to love over to another.

There was a leash around my neck, the choke chain I'd worn the last time Kenyatta took me out, the night of the slave auction. Kenyatta placed the leash in Mistress Delia's hands. I felt like my world was ending. The air suddenly felt too thick to breathe. My chest tightened and my heart raced. I began to hyperventilate.

"No. No, Master! Pleeeease!" I whined, feeling wretched, all self-respect gone. I dropped to my knees and clutched his ankles, kissed his shoes. Kenyatta lifted me back to my feet and tried his best to calm me, holding me close, stroking my hair and whispering softly, but I was inconsolable.

"Shhhhh. It'll be okay, Kitten. I promise. Mistress Delia has a little vineyard and an orchard in Napa. It's beautiful out there. You'll love it. And there will be other slaves so you won't feel so alone."

I shook my head vehemently.

"I don't feel alone! I have you! I don't need anything else. I don't want to be anyone else's slave!"

The blow came suddenly and unexpectedly, catching me off guard and knocking me back against the wall. Kenyatta had slapped me. My face stung from the blow. I was shocked. Yes, I'd been paddled, whipped, spanked, flogged and even caned, but I couldn't remember Kenyatta ever slapping me before, except once or twice during sex. He seized me by the throat and pulled me close so his furious eyes smoldered inches from my own.

"You are a slave. Don't you get that? Do I need to remind you? You are property, a possession, like a pet. I can do with you whatever I wish. I can buy you, sell you, or give you away. Do you understand?"

I nodded. Tears spilled from my eyes.

"Now, I have given you to Mistress Delia and I expect you to behave. Understand?"

Again, I nodded, wiping away tears and fighting back the fit of hysterical weeping threatening to break free. Mistress Delia jerked my leash and I stumbled forward, tripping and falling against her. She dragged me down the steps to her waiting Escalade, popped the rear hatch, and threw me in the back with her dry cleaning and shopping bags.

I hugged my knees to my chest and wept as we pulled out of my Master's driveway. The idea of spending the next few days (Weeks? Months? I didn't know.) away from Kenyatta was terrifying to me. He had been my everything these last few months and now he was simply gone. It was almost inconceivable.

It was a beautiful day. The sun was bright, brilliant, the sky a pale azure with a smattering of wispy cirrus clouds. The city rushed by us in a colorful blur of the city's eclectic denizens, stressed commuters hurrying to the subway or waiting for the bus, joggers sweating in designer workout gear, bicyclists weaving through downtown traffic or racing along the waterfront, shoppers lugging bags stuffed with designers labels, wide-eyed tourists ooohing and aaaahhhing and snapping pictures at all the sights the local residents took for granted, street performers entertaining crowds with frenetic enthusiasm, hippies, hipsters, homosexuals from the flamboyant to the conservative, black, Mexican, and Filipino thugs, and dozens of homeless on every street corner. People of every size, shape, and color filled every available nook of the city. I felt so disconnected from all of them. Their lives were worlds away from mine.

We wound our way through the narrow streets, through the lush verdance of Golden Gate Park, and finally the awe-inspiring beauty of the Golden Gate Bridge itself, overlooking the San Francisco Bay. The bridge had always filled me with awe and wonder. I remembered a description I'd read of the bridge back in high school: "A necklace of surpassing beauty around the lovely throat of San Francisco." That description had always seemed somehow sinister to me. Even then, it brought images of strangulation. Rather than a necklace of jewels, I had always imagined a garrote, cutting off the flow of blood and oxygen to a city struggling to breathe. And now, even as I watched the tranquil flow of sail boats, motorboats, fishing boats, yachts, jet-skiers, and surfers over the dark waters, I felt that same garrote constricting around my own throat.

I struggled to breathe. My own turbulent emotions roiled in contrast with the calm waters below. The crisp clean air choked in my lungs as I watched the tourists who stood on the bridge taking and posing for pictures, joggers and bikers racing toward the Marin Headlands, lovers walking hand in hand, smiling, kissing, laughing, soaking in the sun. I felt lonelier than I could ever recall. Even when I was in the box for hours at a time, I always knew Kenyatta would be home soon to rescue me, feed me, fuck me. Now, I was going who-knows-where to do who-knows-what. For the first time in weeks, I thought about ending the game. I wondered if it had gone too far. I didn't know if I had it in me to continue without seeing Kenyatta every day.

An hour after leaving Kenyatta's house, I was driven to Mistress Delia's home in Napa Valley. I had never seen anything like the vast twenty-two acre estate. It was like stepping into a Hollywood movie. An eleven-acre Cabernet Sauvignon vineyard sprawled out in back of a five-thousand square foot, six bedroom, two-story, custom built Craftsman home with a five-car garage, a 1,200 square foot guest house, and a 4,500 square foot, two-story barn in the back. A lavish rose garden filled the courtyard. It was truly magnificent.

There was a stable and a corral with three horses and two bare-chested men in tight blue jeans. One was white and the other Filipino. They both had athletic builds, not as muscular as Kenyatta, smaller, leaner, but nice...very nice.

I couldn't stop staring at the two stable boys as Mistress Delia opened the hatch of the Escalade and let me out. They both wore thick leather collars around their necks and wrists, making it clear that they were subs, Mistress Delia's property. I wondered how many more slaves she had.

"Come on. I'll have Constance show you to your room. There will be some new clothes for you there."

She led me to the front door, and a tall, slender, light-skinned black woman opened the door dressed similarly to the two boys in the yard. She was topless, wearing a long, flowing, white lace skirt and the same black, leather collar. Her breasts were medium-sized, like two large apples, barely more than a handful, but with large dark nipples. She had wide hips and a slight paunch that somehow made her look even sexier. Just another curve on her lithe, sensuous, body. Her hair was put up in two big Afro puffs on either side of her head. Her smile was wide and genuine with a perfect row of sparkling white teeth framed by soft, pillowy lips. She bowed to Mistress Delia who smiled and kissed her on the lips. Then the woman turned to me and smiled.

"Hi. I'm Constance. Follow me."

She didn't wait for me to introduce myself, before she turned and walked away, revealing a tight and muscular, but still remarkably voluptuous, posterior that jiggled high on her back, putting mine to shame. I guess she must have already known who I was and why I was there. I looked at Mistress Delia who nodded and gestured for me to follow Constance. I was led to a small, sparse room with two bunk beds, two dressers, and one closet. There was an adjoining bathroom, but little else in the way of privacy.

"How many people stay here?" I said.

Constance shrugged. "Depends on the weekend. I'm the only one who stays here permanently. Everyone else is a tourist."

"Tourist" was BDSM slang for those who were less hardcore, who played every now and again, but didn't live the lifestyle twenty-four-seven. Most of the people I knew, including me before the game began, would have fit the definition. I had always questioned the wisdom, and often the sanity, of people who didn't have a clear line between reality and BDSM fantasy role-playing, but now I was one of them.

"Some weekends, we have a full house. The men's quarters hold about five and they can squeeze five or six in here if we double up. Then there are those who come up just for the day. Every so often, we get someone who stays for a whole week or two, and occasionally a month or more. Those tend to be the really rich folks, Europeans on holiday, Japanese businessmen, and the occasional bored millionaire out for a bit of kink. We get a lot of couples here, too."

"So, this isn't just a vineyard then? She's sort of turned it into a little bondage business? A getaway for submissives?"

Constance nodded.

"And doms. If they pay enough. But don't worry. Everything that happens here is safe, sane, and consensual. Even though a client pays, that doesn't guarantee him or her someone to play with. The subs still choose who they want to top them. Sometimes people come here and all they get to do is watch, but they keep coming back."

I tried to imagine someone paying hundreds? Thousands? To live out their fantasy of dominating a willing slave, only to be rejected by every submissive in the house. I would have been pissed. But I had never been much for spectator sports. I always needed to be in the action. That was the best thing about being a submissive. The true power, ultimately lied in the hands of the bottom, "topping from below" as they say. The dom could not do anything the sub didn't want or allow to be done to them. And, usually, a good dom did everything the sub wanted, fulfilled every desire. If they were compatible, their fantasies and desires matched. When they didn't match, there was always a safe word to abort the play. I wondered if I would get a safe word, other than the one Kenyatta had given me.

I put away my simple rags and Constance handed me my new "uniform," a pair of black latex chaps, a red leather G-string, black, leather, open-cup, under bust, corset that lifted my breasts up to my collarbones. She gave me one of the thick, black collars everyone else I'd seen seemed to be wearing, and a long diaphanous white skirt like the one Constance wore. I wondered if she was similarly attired beneath her skirt.

Constance stood by to help me into my new clothes, applying liberal amounts of talc to keep the latex from sticking to my skin. After squeezing, tucking, and stretching myself into it, I had to admit, I felt sexier than I had in months. My breasts were pushed up, ass pushed out, and waist cinched in. All I needed now was someone to admire it all. Again, my mind drifted to Kenyatta, wondering if he was thinking of me and what he would have thought of me in my new outfit. I felt a pang in the core of me, a twinge in my heart. I missed him so much it was painful to think of him, and so, I determined to put Kenyatta out of my mind for as long as I was a guest in Mistress Delia's home.

Constance gave me a head to toe appraisal, looking me over with naked admiration, a mischievous smile on her face and a salacious gleam in her eyes.

"You look wonderful. Really, Natasha. You do. I'd fuck you myself if I had a dick."

I blushed like a virgin schoolgirl and let out an embarrassing high-pitched giggle that left me feeling mortified by my own stupidity.

"Thank you," I mumbled.

Constance smiled, clapped her hands and rubbed them together then pointed toward the door.

"Time to go to work."

I looked down at my outfit.

"What am I supposed to do?"

"You're working in the kitchen with me today. Don't get used to it, though. Tomorrow you're out in the field."

It was an odd outfit for kitchen work, but no odder than Kenyatta insisting that I scrub the floors in the nude. For every bit of historical accuracy Kenyatta insisted on, there was a complimentary dose of his own perversion and fetishism. I had to believe that even his decision to sell me to Delia was another facet of his own fetish. The idea of me at Delia's mercy was a turn-on for him somehow, an extension of his control. Like the slave I was supposed to be, I was his property to buy and sell. If he didn't exercise that power, it was wasted, merely hypothetical. In order for it to be real, for this entire experiment to be more than another perverted sex game, Kenyatta had to sell me. I had to be another's slave. I understood this intellectually, even though it was breaking my heart.

The kitchen was the size of those in the average restaurant, and equally well-equipped. Everything was stainless steel with Sub-Zero and Jenn-Air appliances. In the adjacent dining room, two young doms were drinking wine and talking loudly about the subs they wanted to fuck. Fucking was usually the last thing that went on in these types of places. You played, and if you couldn't get off by whipping or being whipped, then you didn't belong. I knew, because I wasn't sure I belonged. Whippings and paddlings were nice, but I needed a stiff cock or a tongue to get me off.

Constance gave me a big thirty-six quart stainless steel soup pot to cook chili in. I filled it with shredded steak, black beans, and hatch chilies, stirring it with a huge wooden spoon while the two young doms leered at me and the two other girls Constance had brought in to cook with me. One, the head chef, was a tall, voluptuous, Swedish girl with wide hips, large full breasts, and a boisterous smile. She was dressed identically to me, as was the little Filipino girl with the hard, athletic body who was doing all the prep work.

The Swedish woman cooked like she was having the time of her life, that joyous smile seldom leaving her face. Her huge breasts wobbled in the open-cup corset. Her nipples were the size of gumdrops and I couldn't stop staring at them. They were the most beautiful nipples I'd ever seen.

"You can touch them if you like," she said, still smiling with her perfect white teeth.

"W-what?"

"My tits. You like them, yes?"

"They are beautiful."

She turned to face me, thrusting her huge perky breasts toward me. I could see the two men seated in the dining room stir out of the corner of my eye. They were both young Wall Street types. The kind of reckless investors who'd brought the entire economy down risking everything to get rich. They were smug and confident and ogled every woman that passed them. I doubted any of the subs here had allowed either of them near them. Their inexperience radiated like an aura around them. They were the type that went too far and ignored safe words. The kind that would apologize after leaving permanent scars. The kind that secretly hated women. If it weren't for the S&M scene, they would probably have been beating up prostitutes.

I purposely stood in front of the statuesque Swedish girl, blocking the two amateur dom's view as I caressed her perfect breasts. They felt marvelous. The woman smiled and nodded as I squeezed her massive mammaries.

"Your nipples are great," I said.

"You can suck them too," she replied, nodding enthusiastically.

"Really? We won't get in trouble?"

"It's okay. It's okay."

I leaned down, still holding one of her huge mammaries in my hands, and sucked on the big pink nipple. I rolled it around with my tongue and flicked it, feeling it stiffen in my mouth. She moaned softly and held the back of my head, pushing my face into her big, soft, tits.

"Bite them," she said, and I bit down on her nipple. She let out a moan and tilted her head back.

"Harder!"

I bit harder until I felt like I could taste blood.

"That's good. That's good!"

She let out a deep, husky moan. Her body tensed and shivered and she mashed my face harder against her breasts until I was practically suffocating. It took me a moment before I realized she'd been masturbating the entire time I'd been sucking her massive tits. Her hand was between her legs, rubbing her clit with quick, aggressive motions, as if she was punishing herself rather than pleasuring. She sighed, a long satisfied sound, then let go of the back of my head. Her body slumped, relaxed, and she smiled down at me, grateful.

"Thank you," she said then turned and continued working on the slab of beef ribs she was seasoning.

"Don't mention it," I replied as I went back to making the chili.

"What's your name?" I said.

"Suzanna," she replied, still smiling.

"My name is Natasha. I think you owe me one, Suzanna."

Suzanna turned and winked.

"Anytime."

We spent the next few hours in the kitchen, preparing the evening's meal. We made jalapeno cornbread, collard greens, and black-eyed peas in addition to the ribs and chili. A proper country meal.

The subs all ate together at a covered picnic area with big wooden tables and benches, while the doms ate inside in the main dining area. There were ten subs staying there and eight doms. The subs ranged in ages from twenty-two to fifty-seven. Five females and three males. I was surprised to learn that three of the subs were also paying to be there, for the privilege of being abused full-time by professionals. One woman in her mid-forties said she'd been coming here every other weekend for more than three years. She was a lean, athletic woman with close-cropped, sun-bleached blonde hair and a deep tan. She had stern, serious eyes, and it was easy to tell that she was someone of importance in her normal life.

"I've been to farms, dungeons, and chateaus in New York, Los Angeles, London, Paris, and even Tokyo. This is by far my favorite. Not to mention, it's close to home."

There was a man in his fifties who'd also been coming to the farm for years and it took me a moment to figure out that the two were a couple.

"Two subs? How does that work out?"

"It works fine. We take turns topping each other and then we come here whenever we can. We have a perfect relationship."

He was into humiliation, not only being whipped and made to lick women's feet, he also enjoyed being cuckolded, tied up and forced to watch another man fuck his wife.

"Wow." It was all I could think to say. It all seemed so bizarre.

There were two college kids there who worked for the farm, working their way through grad school. Apparently, the fantasy business paid well. I wondered if Kenyatta was paying for me to be there. It now seemed likely and that made me feel better. It meant he was still part of my life, still in control.

After dinner, I helped Suzanna and the quiet Filipino girl, whose name was Patricia, clear all the dishes and wash them. Then we all went to our rooms. I took a shower before going to bed. I was so exhausted I fell asleep with the lights on and the other four girls chatting away like teenagers.

The morning brought a new surprise. Constance arrived with a tight leather outfit complete with leather shorts and a leather open-cup corset. Instead of high heels, this time she handed me a pair of black Doc Marten combat boots. I dressed quickly while Constance stood beside me, tapping her foot impatiently and smiling at some secret joke that I was obviously the butt of. Once I was dressed, she led me out to the wine fields where there was a gray donkey hooked up to an old-fashioned horse plow with two handles and a huge angled, chisel-shaped blade. It sat in the center of a two or three acre patch of land that looked hard and dry, as if it had never grown anything and never would.

"Mistress needs you to plow this field. You're not working in the kitchen anymore. You're a field nigger now. Make sure the lines are straight."

With that, she turned and headed back to the house.

"Wait! I've never done this before. I don't know how."

"Well, you'd better figure it out. Here." She handed me a buggy whip. "Seymore can be a little stubborn sometimes. Just give him a crack every now and then to keep him moving. The rows should be nine to ten feet apart and twenty-four inches deep. Oh, and there will be a couple overseers coming by in a few hours to check on you. Have fun."

I was left standing there with the buggy whip, staring at the donkey and plow with no clue what to do with either of them. I clomped over and took hold of the plow. I gave the mule a crack with the buggy whip and he began to move forward, the plow fell over and took me with it.

"Shit!" I exclaimed loudly as I climbed back to my feet and wiped dirt from my legs and arms. I struggled to lift the heavy plow back up, and this time, I held on tight, straining to keep it straight as the donkey moved forward. My arms shook as I struggled to steady the plow. My shoulders and back sang out in pain almost immediately from the exertion. Worse, I couldn't keep the plow straight. It bounced and jerked, shaking my entire body, my breasts bounced and flopped like I was jogging without a bra and ripples ran up my ass and thighs. I could barely hold onto the plow. The lines in the soil meandered all over the place. The plow was just so heavy, it was all I could do to keep it from falling over again.

I finished the first row. It was a mess that resembled a parenthesis more than a straight line. I started the next row, determined to do better this time, but met with only slightly more success. I stumbled over the churned earth and rocks as I scrambled along behind the mule, fighting the plow, struggling to keep it in a straight line as it cut through the dirt. The plow jerked and jostled as the mule pulled, bumping and rattling over the rocks and hard packed earth, jarring my entire body, threatening to jolt from my grip.

After more than an hour behind the plow, I was finally getting the hang of it, managing to make rows that were relatively straight. That's when the two young asshats from the dining room, who'd been salivating while I fondled Suzanna's breasts, rode up on horses carrying cat o' nine tails.

"What the fuck are you doing? This looks like shit!"

The guy who spoke was the whitest white boy she could have imagined, the personification of a White Anglo-Saxon Protestant yuppie, even in black leather. When he wasn't playing dom, she imagined he wore polo shirts, cardigans, and argyle socks. He had neatly quaffed blond hair, blue eyes, a wide mouth with thin lips that looked like someone had sliced a hole in his face, a weak chin, narrow shoulders, and no discernible muscles. His body was thin where it should have been thick and thick where it should have been thin, skinny arms and legs, a paunch, and love handles that were starting to become hips.

He regarded me like I was something in his toy box. There was no recognition of my humanity at all in his eyes. His cruel expression and lustful eyes said clearly what he thought of me and likely all women. I was an object, something to be fucked and abused then put away until it was time to fuck again. As far as I was concerned, he fit only the loosest interpretation of the word "man."

The guy riding along behind him was olive-skinned and athletically built with short, wavy black hair.

"You're going to have to do this all over again," he said in a clipped Middle-Eastern accent that brought out all of my own prejudices, automatically assuming he was a conservative Muslim who thought all women were beneath him. But what would a conservative Muslim be doing at an S&M fantasy plantation? I had no answer.

I looked back over the work I'd done and there was no denying it. The earth looked like it had been scarred rather than tilled. I looked over at a nearby patch of land where grapevines grew in neat, orderly rows, then back at the meandering rows I'd carved into the earth. It did indeed look like shit. I had left six uneven rows that were as close as five or six feet apart in spots and as wide as twelve feet in others, and I had exhausted myself doing it. Still, I wanted to tell these two assholes to fuck themselves, but that wasn't my place. That would have been asking for a whipping. I bowed my head and averted my eyes.

I took a deep breath, cracked the whip, and picked up the ends of the plow. That's when Seymore decided to show his stubborn streak. He sat down in the center of the field.

"Yah! Yah, Seymore! Come on, you stupid donkey! Don't do this to me!"

The two douche bags climbed down off their horses. I rolled my eyes, anticipating the coming ridicule and abuse.

"Did you hear what we said? Get going and fix this abomination!"

The Muslim cracked the cat o' nine tails he carried across my hamstrings. The tails wrapped around the front, leaving livid, red welts on my thighs. I gritted my teeth and tried again to get Seymore moving. The WASP walked toward me with a deeply affected look of anger on his face that was meant to intimidate, but only managed to make him look even more ridiculous, like a boy pretending to be a man. He wore a full leatherman outfit, chaps and all, over a pair of blue jeans and a white t-shirt. He pointed the cat at my face as he barked orders at me.

"I said, get to work and fix this shit! Do you want me to tell Mistress Delia what you've done to her land?"

I doubted she would care. If she gave a damn about this particular parcel of land, she certainly wouldn't have placed it in my inexperienced hands. I didn't reply and I didn't look at the ridiculous boy/man. Instead, I tried to imagine an African slave on a Southern plantation, being faced with the same dilemma, a difficult and unfamiliar task and the threat of severe physical punishment if it wasn't done perfectly. It was something millions of slaves had likely endured, and I would endure it too.

I tried again to get Seymore moving and again, he remained stubbornly seated. The WASP began whipping me relentlessly, striping my back, arms, ass, and thighs with the cat. He made so much commotion that Seymore finally stood and began to move forward. I grabbed the handles of the plow and guided him back over the same land we'd just plowed, but the two assholes weren't done. The Muslim guy grabbed my arms and the WASP tried to rip off my corset.

"Get off of me! What are you doing?"

"We're not done with you, bitch! You need to be punished. But I tell you what, you suck us both off, let us give you a nice bukakke shower, and we'll let you go," the WASP said, grinning at his Muslim buddy like the wild-eyed frat boy he'd probably been not long ago.

"You must be fucking high! Get the fuck off of me!"

"Hold her, Farad! Hold her still!"

"She's fighting, man. I don't think she's playing."

"I don't care. We paid our money, we're fucking someone! No way anyone is going to cry rape at an S&M club. It would get laughed out of court. I'm fucking this cunt if she likes it or not! Now, hold her still!"

His hands were all over me, pawing at my breasts. I kicked at him, and he slapped me so hard I saw stars. That's when I screamed.

"Heeeelllp! Raaaape! Raaaaape!"

This time, he punched me. His fist caught me behind the left ear and the world spun. I found myself staring up at the sky. Someone was tugging my shorts down and I looked up to see the WASP standing above me, unzipping his pants. I tried to scream again. The Muslim clamped a hand over my mouth and I bit it. I bit deep and jerked my head to the side, ripping a chunk out of his hand just below his pinky. He yelled and jumped backwards. I sat up quickly, still feeling woozy, and grabbed blindly for the WASP's penis the instant it poked from his zipper. The man jumped backwards, but it was too late. My fingernails sunk into his cock. I dug them in deep, seizing his cock and twisting it. The WASP howled and struck me again, punching me in the top of my head. I leaned forward and jerked him toward me, dragging him by his penis.

"Fuck! Let go! Let go, you fucking bitch!" he shouted as I pulled him closer, tugging and wrenching on his cock, wringing it like a dishrag. I sank my teeth into his nutsack, biting down hard and feeling his testes rupture in my mouth like hardboiled eggs. His screams were horrific. He punched at my head and I could feel myself beginning to lose consciousness, but I refused. I bit down harder, biting through his scrotum. I could hear footsteps hurrying toward us as I ripped and tore at the WASP's flaccid sex organs, tearing his testicles from his body and trying to pull his cock free from its moorings. Blood, urine, and semen rained down his thighs and dripped from my mouth as I chewed up his testicles and spit them down into the dirt.

"What's going on?" I heard someone shout, followed by the unmistakable dull smack of knuckles striking flesh and a body thudding down in the dirt with a loud "Oof!"

I looked around for my savior. It was Constance along with the two male subs with the perfect bodies I'd seen in the stables the day I arrived.

"They tried to rape me!"

The Muslim guy, Farad, was on his knees next to Constance, flanked by the two subs. He cradled his wounded hand. His eye was swelling shut, his lip was busted, and his jaw hung at an odd angle. They had kicked his ass before they even knew what he'd done. His face held a pitiful expression, like a cornered rat.

"I-I didn't do anything!" he protested.

Constance whirled around to face the cowed and conquered Muslim guy and he cringed. Without a hint of hesitation, she kicked him in the chest, aiming her four-inch stiletto heel at his heart like she was trying to impale him on it. He pitched backward into the dirt and remained there, holding his chest and wincing. A trickle of blood leaked out from between his fingers.

The WASP was lying on his back, trembling. His eyes rolled back in his head, then swam back into focus briefly before rolling up again. He looked like he was going to die.

Good! I thought, and spit at his prone form. The two subs walked over and began kicking and stomping him in the face with their pointy-toed cowboy boots until blood leaked from his mouth and ears. Constance stared down at him with hard, unfeeling eyes, then she leaned over and gathered me up in her arms.

"Don't worry, he's not going to be hurting anyone else for a long time."

CHAPTER XI

Mistress Delia drove me to the hospital in her Escalade. My head and jaw hurt from where that asshole had punched me and the coppery, meaty taste of his blood and flesh lay thick on my tongue.

"Don't worry about anything. I told the police what happened. Both of those assholes are being charged with attempted rape. Sorry, I didn't get there sooner. Nothing like this has happened at the farm before," Mistress Delia said. She was dressed conservatively in jeans and a sweatshirt that hid all her sensuality and made her look like just another fat chick. I felt bad for her and curiously protective of her, even in my own damaged state. I didn't want people thinking my Mistress was anything less than the beautiful woman I knew her to be.

"They want you to have a rape kit performed."

"But-but, I wasn't raped."

"You said, you blacked out for a second and when you woke up, one of them was holding you down and the other one had his penis out. You may have been out longer than you realize. Something may have happened. The police have your clothes to test for semen."

I looked down at myself and only then realized that I was wearing different clothing. I had on a simple, white sundress. It was only then that I realized how much time had passed since Kenyatta and I began this game. It had been autumn when he took me to the slave auction and now spring was in full bloom. I had barely noticed the passing of the seasons, trapped in my own private hell.

"They are going to ask you about the winery, what you were doing out there alone. Plowing a field dressed in a leather corset. They're going to try to turn this into some kinky sex thing. What are you going to tell them?"

"I'll tell them I was helping you out with some farming. I was dressed like that because I was on private property and I can dress any way I damn well please and how I dress shouldn't have shit to do with why these two assholes tried to rape me!"

Mistress nodded.

We pulled up to the hospital's Emergency Room entrance and a police officer opened my door. They had followed us to the hospital. Apparently Mistress Delia had insisted on driving me herself and wouldn't let them put me in an ambulance. I could only assume she'd wanted to ensure I wouldn't say anything to jeopardize her business while I was out of her sight. I preferred to believe she'd done it out of concern for me.

As I stepped from Mistress's big SUV into a waiting wheelchair, she whispered to me.

"Uh, do you want me to call Kenyatta?"

It was an odd question. Of course I wanted Kenyatta to know I was in the hospital. I wanted him to come and hold me in his powerful arms, let me cry on his strong shoulders. I wanted him to punish those two assholes. The beating Constance and her goons had given them wasn't enough. I wanted to see them humbled. I wanted my man to show them what a real man was. But something about the way she asked it made me pause. Would Kenyatta be angry at me for what happened? Would the experiment be over and what would that mean? Would he still marry me or not? I had no idea, no answers.

"Uh, um. Maybe we should wait a while."

Mistress nodded as an ER nurse led me away with the police officer at my side.

I felt numb, physically and emotionally as the nurse swabbed my mouth, vagina, and anus for DNA samples and inspected each orifice for bruising. My cuts and bruises were treated then photographed by a victim's advocate from the police department. Eventually I was led to my room to recover.

Before I was allowed to rest, I was interviewed by a police detective from the SFPD sex crimes unit along with the victim's advocate, a plump and pleasant Latino woman in her late twenties.

"Are you feeling okay to talk?" the woman said.

I nodded.

"My name is Eileen Gonzalez and this is Detective Watkins from Sex Crimes. We have a few questions for you and then we'll leave you alone and let you get some rest. You've been through a lot today. Would you tell us what happened?"

"I was helping Misstre—Miss Delia plow the field for her new grape vines when two of her other guests rode up on horseback and started teasing me and asking me to have sex with them."

I saw the detective exchange a look with Eileen that was thick with judgment. He knew what kind of place Mistress Delia ran and had already decided that I'd been asking to be raped. It was all my fault. He probably thought the two assholes I'd bitten were the real victims.

"What kind of things did they say?" Detective Watkins said. The detective was a middle-aged, fireplug-shaped black man with thick muscular arms and shoulders, a big belly, and a growing bald spot in the center of his close-cropped, salt and pepper hair. His face had no wrinkles, but the lines around his mouth and those in his forehead were etched deep from years of worry.

"They said that I fucked up the field, that it looked like shit and I should give them both blowjobs to make up for the shitty job I'd done working the plow. It was my first time working a plow and I didn't make the rows straight. I tried, but I couldn't get the hang of it."

"That's okay. It's okay," Eileen said. "Then what happened?"

"I told them to go fuck themselves and then they attacked me. They started groping my breasts and then they tried to rip my clothes off. When I fought back, they punched me. The white guy knocked me down with a punch. I think I went out for a little bit."

"Went out? You mean you were knocked unconscious?" the detective said.

"Yes."

"When did he expose himself to you?"

"What? Oh, I was waking up after he knocked me out and he was standing above me, pulling his cock out of his pants."

"Then what did you do?"

"I screamed rape, but that Arab bastard put his hand over my mouth. So I bit him. I bit his hand."

"What happened then?"

"Then I looked back at the white guy and he had his cock completely out of his pants and was coming at me with it, so I grabbed it and tried to rip it off. Then he started punching me again, so I bit him. I tried to bite his nuts off."

"You did," the detective answered without looking up from his notepad where he was scribbling down my account of the assault.

"What?"

"The guy's nuts, you bit them completely off. You almost tore his dick off. He's gonna need reconstructive surgery. I doubt he'll ever work right down there again."

"Fuck that piece of shit. I hope he has to piss out his asshole," I hissed, my years of education slipping away and my white trash origins reemerging.

Eileen, the victim's advocate, nodded. Not in agreement but in understanding. I wasn't sure whether she was patronizing me or not.

"Why were you wearing this to plow a field?" the detective said, holding up an oversized Ziploc bag with the leather corset and short shorts I'd been wearing.

I smirked and shook my head.

"I was wondering when you were going to ask. You know what kind of place it is. People go there to live out their sexual fantasies."

The detective nodded then locked eyes with me.

"And wasn't that just what these two guys were doing? Weren't they just playing out their fantasies?"

I scowled and shook my head.

"No. There are rules. Everything has to be consensual. That policy is strictly enforced. We all sign a contract. You can't just grab whoever you want and rape them just because they're wearing a sexy outfit. That's bullshit!"

The detective nodded again.

"And what exactly was your fantasy?"

I opened my mouth to speak then reconsidered. The truth wasn't likely to help my case. It was more likely to further alienate the detective from me, convince him that I was a lunatic.

"It's personal."

The advocate sighed.

"We are only asking because, if you pursue charges against these two, and I think you should, they're going to ask you all of this."

"My fantasy wasn't to be raped in the dirt by two yuppies, if that's what you're asking."

Eileen blushed.

"I—no—that's not what I meant."

"What she means is that something like wanting to be part of a gang bang or even certain types of rough sex, might help them make the case that they were led on."

"Led on? Like I wanted to be beaten up?"

"Where did you get the welts on your back? Some of those scars look pretty old."

"Oh, so you're saying that because I like to get whipped, I might like to get punched too? Maybe I was asking for it? Fuck you, detective! Get the fuck out of here!"

"We have to ask."

That was all the detective said as he closed his notebook and stood.

"Get out! Both of you!"

Eileen smiled and placed her business card beside me on the nightstand.

"Call me if you need to talk."

I snatched her card off the table, ripped it in half, and threw it at her. Then the phone rang. I snatched it up, hoping it was Kenyatta, ready to pour out my misery to him and have him make it all better with a few soothing words. For him to say he was on his way to rescue me, take me home. Love me. But it wasn't him. It was an angry spiteful voice, the voice of the man who'd tried to fuck me against my will.

"You'd better tell them it wasn't rape, bitch! You hear me? Do you know how much I'm worth? How much my family's worth? I've got the best goddamn lawyers in the city and what the fuck have you got? You were at a fucking fetish farm! The jury is going to say you were asking for it because you were. You know you were, you fucking slut! You wanted it. Why the fuck else were you there? What did you expect? They'll all call you a whore! Whores deserve to get raped. That's what they'll say."

I don't know why it took me so long to hang up the phone. My hand was shaking when I did and tears were streaming down my face. I should have told the police about the call. I should have had him rearrested, his bail revoked, but I just felt so exhausted and ashamed. Very ashamed. What the fuck was I doing there? Why had Kenyatta sent me there? Why was I doing any of this? I was thinking about what the asshole on the phone said. *"They'll all call you a whore. Whores deserve to get raped."* I was thinking about the trial ahead. And all I wanted to do was sleep. Where was Kenyatta? Where was my protector? I closed my eyes, and cried until the dreams faded to black.

CHAPTER XII

Kenyatta could not believe what he was hearing. Someone had dared to touch his woman, his property.

"Who are they? Where do they live? Are they regulars?"

"This was their first time at the farm."

Kenyatta put both hands on Delia's shoulders and squeezed gently, but firmly, compelling Delia to meet his stern gaze.

"Delia." Kenyatta relaxed his features, letting the tension out of his expression, forcing a smile as he brushed the hair from her face and caressed her cheek with his palms and fingertips. He cradled her face in his hands, gently, like he was holding something delicate, precious, invaluable. He licked his lips. Then kissed her lightly on the mouth. He could feel Delia tremble in his grasp. Cruelty she could take. She was part of an industry of staged, consensual fantasy violence. In her world, violence was something passionate, even romantic, but she knew he could see it in her eyes, she knew that the cruelty in his eyes, though passionate, would be neither romantic nor consensual. "Tell me."

"I-I don't know what you want."

"Yes you do. You wouldn't let strangers stay at your home unless you checked them out."

"I have their name and credit card on file as well as their billing address but—"

"Give it to me."

"King..."

"Give it to me!"

CHAPTER XIII

Farad Ali sat at the bar, the same bar he and his frat brothers used to frequent in college. A table on the other side of the room was filled with young kids from his old fraternity. He didn't know any of them and they didn't know him. The oldest of them was probably still in high school when Farrad had graduated. Still, he felt a kinship with them. He and his friends used to sit at that same table talking about the same teachers, classes, parties, what girls he'd fucked, would fuck, wished he could fuck, how much money he would make when he graduated, how he'd buy a condo with a view of the bay, and what kind of bad-ass bitch-magnet he would drive and all the high quality pussy he would get because of it. All the shit these fools were shouting loudly back and forth to each other. Farrad knocked back another shot of tequila.

On any other day, he might have gone over to that table and showed them the Greek letters branded on his bicep. He would have told them that he was the one who'd put the brass Buddha with "Fat Fuck" stenciled on his belly in "The Fat Room" and made it a tradition to stick it outside the door whenever you were in there fucking someone you normally wouldn't be caught dead with. Then they would swap stories about the chicks they'd done in that room. But not today. Today he sat at the bar, head down, shoulders hunched, casting nervous glances at the TV behind the bar, hoping his picture wouldn't suddenly flash on the screen with the caption: "Accused Rapist in Sex Farm Scandal" emblazoned on the screen below it.

I can't believe I let Michael talk me into this shit, Farrad thought. *My life is ruined!* "Bartender! Line up another shot!"

There was a large black man sitting across the bar facing him. He was dressed all in black; black, buttoned-down, short-sleeved shirt, black jeans, even wearing black leather gloves and dark sunglasses that wrapped around his head like *The Terminator.* His muscles bulged through his shirt like Arnold Schwarzenegger, and the man appeared to be staring right through Farrad, but he couldn't be certain because of the opaque sunglasses. Farrad tried to stare back, but when the man didn't turn away, Farrad averted his eyes. He didn't want to be the one to start shit with a guy that huge. He had enough trouble without getting his ass kicked in a bar fight.

Farrad continued to drink, growing increasingly suspicious of the man in the dark sunglasses. He could feel his bravery increasing with each shot of tequila.

I should ask this guy what his fucking problem is, Farrad thought, but he wasn't quite drunk enough for that. He asked the bartender for his bill and settled his tab, then staggered toward the door. He cast a glance behind him as he opened the door and stepped out into the night. The large black man in the sunglasses had turned his head toward him. Now there was no question whether the guy was staring at him.

"What the fuck are you lookin' at?" Farrad yelled, then turned and rushed out into the street before the man could reply, fearing the huge man would come after him. Once he was outside in the parking lot, he wondered why he thought he'd be safer out here than inside where there were witnesses. He stumbled over to his vehicle and fumbled his keys out of his pocket and into his car door, looking over his shoulder to make certain the man wasn't coming after him. Once Farrad had opened the car and slumped behind the wheel, feeling the madness of the day and the alcohol coalesce into a deep existential malaise, he let out an exhausted sigh and looked back toward the bar. His blood pressure spiked. He could feel his heart pounding in his ears.

The big black guy was standing outside the bar, staring across the parking lot directly at him. The man began walking toward him.

"Oh shit!"

Farrad jammed the key in the ignition and started the car. The man in the sunglasses reached for his car door. Farrad stomped down on the accelerator, spitting bits of gravel and asphalt from his tires as he drove out of the parking lot, flipping the big guy in the sunglasses the finger as he pulled out into the street. He breathed a long sigh of relief when he could see the man in his rear view mirror, shrinking in the distance. Farrad's BMW

Z4 convertible sports car roared down the road and he thrust both of his middle fingers into the air.

"Fuck Yooooooou!"

He didn't see the man climb into the black Chrysler 300 and follow his vehicle down the road.

When Farrad pulled into the underground parking garage at his high-rise condominium, he didn't notice the Chrysler pull in behind him, reversing the electric gate before it could close. Farrad was still pitying his bad luck, getting involved in an attempted rape, being arrested, wondering how he would explain it all to his employers, if he would lose his job. When he stepped from his car he was trying to think of a story to tell his fiancée, who didn't know about his predilection for sadism, but thought he had gone on a fishing trip with some old college buddies. Then something struck the back of his head, the ground rushed up to meet his face, and everything went black.

Farrad had a lovely dream in which he and Michael hadn't tried to rape the girl with the huge tits, but she'd willingly given herself to them instead, crawling to them with a whip clenched between her teeth, begging them to use it on her, just like he'd imagined it would be at the farm. And after she'd been whipped into submission, she'd begged them both to fuck her, and they'd taken her in both holes, double penetration, Farrad raping her asshole while Michael fucked her from the front. It was quite a wonderful dream, until Farrad was awakened by a slap across his face.

"Wake up, motherfucker! Time to play!"

Farrad was naked and bound. It took him a moment to orient himself. His head hurt and he was dizzy, but he knew the feel of leather, and he couldn't move his arms or legs. There were restraints around his wrists and ankles, but that wasn't the worst of it. He was wrapped from head to toe in plastic; mummified.

"Wh—" He tried to speak. But there was something gagging him. He tasted latex and felt something long and thick filling his mouth, almost touching the back of his throat to the point where he would have gagged and probably thrown up and drowned on his own vomit, but not quite there. It didn't take him long to figure out what it was in his mouth either—a dildo. Someone had shoved a dildo in his mouth.

There was something over his eyes, and that increased Farrad's terror. Immobilized, gagged, and blindfolded, the voice that had woken him up did not sound friendly. It sounded downright pissed-da-fuck-off.

"You and your buddy like to rape women? Well, tonight you're my woman!"

That didn't sound good either.

Farrad couldn't feel anything. The plastic wrapped around him from wrists to ankles, cut off all sensation, at least until his captor cut a small, six-inch square in the plastic, right below his navel. Then he felt the unmistakable sting of a razor blade. He'd been cut before, but it had never hurt like this. With all his other cutaneous senses numbed, he had no choice but to concentrate on the pain, the pain and the malevolent growl of his captor. Farrad tried to scream, but the effort seemed to make the dildo slide further into his throat and he almost choked. The cutting continued, it felt like he was being eviscerated. The pain was excruciating, his guts twisted in knots and Farrad imagined his torturer had cut open his belly and was squeezing his intestines with bare hands. Then another spot was cut open. This one on his chest, right where his nipple was or rather, where it had been. This time, Farrad did scream, despite the dildo in his mouth. He emptied his lungs, inhaled, then screamed again, a shrill, high-pitched sound he'd have never imagined himself capable of. It didn't fit at all with his self-image of a strong, successful alpha male with all the opportunity for success a mere arm's length away. This was the sound a woman made. And he made it again, when his torturer cut away another square of plastic, right over his groin.

Farrad had never been circumcised. That wasn't something they did in his culture. But in a matter of a few agonizing minutes that made Farrad wish he was still unconscious, still locked behind bars, or even dead, his torturer relieved him of his foreskin. He had turned him from a Muslim to a Jew, but thankfully, not a eunuch. Then Farrad felt something else that made him scream even louder than before, that made him pray to Allah to save him. A large square was cut from around his buttocks and something cool, wet, and slippery was slathered on his rectum. Lubricant. Astroglide by the smell of it. There was no mistaking it for anything else.

"I told you I was going to make you my woman. Let's see you tell the cops what I did to you. Tell them you were kidnapped and raped. Then, every time someone, a friend, co-worker, employer, girlfriend does a web search on your name, that's what will come up, that you got raped by another man. See, if I just kicked your ass, you could tell someone you got sucker-punched. You could tell them you got jumped by a bunch of guys."

Farrad could sense the man leaning over his shoulder, then he felt the man's hands on his hips, felt something hard, long, and thick, part his ass cheeks and thrust deep into his bowels. Farrad cried. He wept from the pain and humiliation as his asshole was rhythmically violated.

"But are you going to tell them that you were raped? You going to tell them a man came in your ass? Is that what you want following you for the rest of your life, accused rapist and rape victim? Oh, and what if you get convicted and go to prison? Do you know what will happen to you if all those inmates know that you were raped? You'll be getting raped every day. But, if you want to go to the cops, I'll make sure there are enough DNA samples if you really want to press charges. I'll make sure there's no doubt what was done to you."

He felt the man's cock thicken, felt the hard body pressed against his backside go rigid, and then he felt the warm explosion in his loins as his attacker ejaculated inside him. Farrad could not stop crying. When his violator began to beat him, punching and kicking him, Farrad was beyond caring. He hoped the man would kill him.

CHAPTER XIV

"Fuck that bitch! My lawyers will eat her alive. That fucking slut won't get a dime from me!"

"She's not after money, Michael. She's pressing criminal charges. You're going to be tried for attempted rape."

"That's bullshit! We were in a sex club! On a goddamn S&M farm for Christsakes! She wouldn't have been there if she didn't want to get fucked!"

Michael's father shook his head, placing his palm against his forehead and closing his eyes.

"Something is not right with you, Michael."

Michael smirked.

"I'm just fine, Dad."

"No, you're not. You need to see a therapist, a psychiatrist. I'm not going to have my son turn into some kind of rapist or serial sex murderer or something!"

"You're overreacting, Dad. Me and Farrad just went to a fetish farm to check it out and see what it was like. Chicks go there to live out their fantasies of being overpowered and dominated. I was just giving that bitch what she wanted. Who knew she was going to freak out like that? It doesn't matter anyway. I told you, I've already got a lawyer on this. Nothing is going to happen. You'll see. I might even sue that bitch for what she did to my sack. They had to sew it back on!"

Michael Evans Sr. looked his son in his eyes, placed his palm against the boy's cheek, then ran a hand through his own thinning hair, before dropping his head into his palms and letting out a sigh that appeared to empty his body of all vitality. He wilted into the brown leather recliner he was sitting in, looking as if he'd aged thirty years in a matter of seconds.

"Maybe something should happen. Maybe you should go to jail."

"Dad!"

Michael looked at his father.

"You don't mean that."

Michael Sr. seemed to diminish even further, folding into the plush brown leather recliner, collapsing in on himself.

"Maybe I don't."

Michael nodded. He patted his weary father on his stooped shoulders.

"It'll be okay, Dad. You'll see."

Michael bent and kissed the bald spot on his father's bowed head, turned and left the room. He snatched a thin windbreaker from the coat rack, protection against the chill breeze and late night fog. It still amazed him that it could be seventy degrees during the day and drop into the forties at night when the fog rolled in. To Michael, the weather in San Francisco was every bit as fickle as its citizens. He grabbed a bottle of

Grey Goose vodka off the bar, took a swig, and carried it out with him to his car.

Michael's cell phone rang as he stepped from the apartment and hurried to the black Porsche parked at the curb.

"Yeah?"

"It's Farrad."

His voice sounded hoarse, weak. Farrad trembled, choking back sobs. Michael had never heard his friend sound so…weak, so defeated. Pussy. Some guys just couldn't take the heat. Threaten them with prison and they fell the fuck apart.

"What's up, bro? You all freaked out about getting arrested? I told you, my lawyers are the best in the business. They are handling it."

There was a pause. A strangled sob. Then a whisper.

"Someone…a big black guy…he attacked me. He…he…did things to me."

"What kind of things? What are you talking about? Where are you?"

"I'm in the hospital. Watch out, man. Be careful. I-I think he might be coming for you too. I think it has something to do with that whore from the fetish farm. I gotta go. The cops are here."

The phone died and Michael immediately turned, expecting someone to be creeping up behind him. The street was empty. He climbed into the car, slammed the door shut, locked it, and shifted the Porsche into drive. Only then did he feel the chill breeze on the back of his neck. His hairs stood on end and icy tendrils of fear clawed his spine.

Michael turned and noticed two things simultaneously. His rear passenger window had been busted out and there was someone in the back seat...someone very large with a knife. Michael jerked forward, startled, terrified. He pulled the door handle and stepped one leg out onto the pavement. That was as far as he got. The man grabbed him by his hair and jerked him back into the seat. Michael yelled. His cry choked off suddenly when he felt the cold steel against his Adam's apple.

"Shut up and drive."

"Don't kill me!"

The blade cut into his skin and Michael yelped. A warm wet trickle dribbled down his neck.

"If you don't shut that fucking door and put your foot on the gas, I'm going to give you a second smile. You got that shit?" The voice was deep, gravely, angry. It didn't have a hint of bluff in it. If anything, it sounded like the man was doing everything he could to restrain himself from slitting Michael's throat.

Michael obeyed, closing the door and driving farther into the park. The man frisked him quickly, roughly. Michael wept like a child.

"No gun? You're a cocky son of a bitch ain't you? You rape a woman and it never even occurs to you that someone might want to retaliate?"

"D-d-don't h-h-h-h-hurt me, duuuude. This was...this was just a misunderstanding. I didn't mean to hurt her. We were all just having fun. She wanted it. I'm telling you, she wanted it."

There was silence from the back seat. Michael looked into the rearview mirror and could only see a dark silhouette, a shadow that was darker and more solid than the other shadows.

"You hear me, dude? I didn't do shit!"

"Don't call me dude. Turn left right here, motherfucker."

The man guided him through a series of turns down familiar streets, finally leading him into Golden Gate Park.

"No way, man. I'm not going in there!"

"I'm going to make this real simple, Michael. If you do as I say, I won't kill you. I'm going to hurt you. I'm going to hurt you a lot. But I won't kill you. But if you fuck with me. If you don't do exactly what I say, I'm going to gut you like a fish. You've only got a few seconds to decide how this is going to go. Then I start making you bleed. I didn't kill your little sidekick and I could have. But I promise you, if you don't do exactly as I say, I will cut your fucking head off, slice open your belly, and decorate this nice eighty-thousand dollar sports car with your internal organs. Now, drive!"

Michael stepped on the accelerator and piloted the Porsche into the park.

"Turn off your headlights."

"But...I won't be able to see the road."

"There's a full moon. You can see just fine. Turn off your fucking headlights."

Michael began to tremble. He felt some mild relief knowing the man hadn't killed Farrad. Whatever this man had done to him, Farrad was still alive. It had been less than an hour since Michael had spoken to him. But Farrad said the man had done "things" to him. That's how Farrad had put it. "Things." As if whatever was done to him had been too terrible to verbalize.

Sobs escaped Michael's quivering lips. He began to snivel and weep as his imagination conjured up visions of castration and other, more terrible forms of genital torture. He'd once seen a picture in a body modification magazine of a man who'd had his penis split in half, a row of rings pierced through each side. Michael's testicles shriveled up tight against him, a whimper escaped from his lips.

"Stop the car."

They were in an area of the park that wasn't visible from the main road. The dense trees and other foliage formed a thick canopy that blocked out the stars and moon. The streetlights didn't reach this far, so the darkness was absolute. No one would see them and no one would hear them. Michael could hear the sound of crashing waves from the San Francisco Bay. It was an isolated, lonely sound. A hopeless sound.

"Please don't do this. Don't do this!"

The back door opened and Michael began to cry as the huge black man with a very large knife wrenched up his door and dragged him out of the car by his hair, punching him in the face repeatedly as he pulled him down into the dirt. Michael's face cut, bled, bruised, and swelled.

"Please. Please. Please. No. No. No. Noooooo!"

The punches weren't the worst of it. Once out of the car, the man began cutting off Michael's clothes.

Michael tried to resist, but each attempt to protect himself was met with punches that made the world spin. Michael blacked out several times. The last time, he awoke to find himself naked, face down, duct tape around his wrists and ankles, the huge black man violating his anus with the hilt of the huge buck knife. Michael screamed as the man rammed the leather-coated knife handle deep in his bowels without any lubricant but his own brute force. It felt like his anus was being cored out like an apple. Blood squished from his rectum and ran down the sides of his buttocks as the man continued to rape him with the knife. The duct tape around Michael's mouth muffled the sound of his agonized screams, not that anyone would have heard him this deep in Golden Gate Park.

The man dragged a large duffel bag out of the car and withdrew a baseball bat, then he reached back in and took out the bottle of Grey Goose Michael had brought with him from his father's bar. He withdrew the knife from Michael's anus and replaced it with bottle of Grey Goose, easing it in deeper and deeper, using Michael's own blood and feces as lubricant. Michael's guts cramped as he felt the cool, glass, bottle fill his vandalized rectum. Then the man rose, placed a foot on the small of Michael's back for leverage and to hold Michael in place, then lifted the bat. Michael screamed and tried to squirm away, knowing what was about to happen next. The man swung the bat down hard, hammering the bottle into his colon and shattering it.

What felt like a hundred shards of glass embedded themselves deep in Michael's hemorrhoidal tissue. Then the man used the business end of the bat to grind the glass in deeper, putting his shoulders into it and grunting audibly with the effort. He shoved the bat in as deep as he could, managing to get nearly six inches of it into Michael's anus, rupturing blood vessels as jagged shards were embedded deep into his rectum. Before climbing back in the car, the man urinated all over Michael, taking care to aim the warm stream at Michael's face.

Michael was still conscious, screaming in a hell of indescribable pain, when the man leaned down and whispered in his ear. The man's face was all shadow. Eyes and a mouth surrounded by darkness that bled into the surrounding night. It took a moment for Michael to realize what he was looking at. A ski mask. His attacker was wearing some sort of black Lycra ski mask.

"I could have castrated you permanently. I should have castrated you. You will not fight this in court. Even if you tell the police what I did to you. Even if they catch me, one of my dear friends will come to visit you, and they will take from you, whatever I want them to take. Cut it off and bring it to me. Do you understand?"

Michael nodded, still sobbing and sniveling.

"If you fight the charges in court. If you try to make Natasha out to be some kind of slut who asked to be raped. I will be angry. I will come for you again. Do you understand?"

Again, Michael nodded.

"Now, when you get to a phone, I want you to call the hospital, ask for Natasha, and I want you to apologize to her. I want you to beg her to forgive you. If you don't, I will come for you again. You understand, you piece of shit?"

"Yes! Yes, I understand! Don't hurt me again! Don't kill me!"

The man in the black mask climbed into Michael's car and drove away, leaving Michael naked in the park with the baseball bat still protruding from his bleeding asshole.

CHAPTER XV

The phone rang and every nerve vibrated in sync with the chime. I wanted to scream. My head was cloudy from the pain meds, but the pain was still there, pounding like thunder between my ears. A migraine the magnitude of Mount St. Helens.

I remembered where I was. Why I was there. Attempted rape. It was an old story, but one I thought I'd put behind me. Meeting Kenyatta was supposed to mean the end of drunken date rapes. He was supposed to keep me safe, but he hadn't been there to protect me.

Hours passed. Nurses came and went, checking my vitals, asking me how I felt and whether I needed something for my nerves. I watched soap operas and game shows. A psychiatrist came in, looked at my chart, then asked me if I was having nightmares, trouble sleeping, if I would be afraid to leave the hospital and go home, and then, finally, the big question: "Have you had any suicidal thoughts?"

I laughed. I don't know why. I just thought it was funny. Almost every day of my life, the idea of suicide had been there. I even found it comforting to know there was always a way out of this madness if it got too rough.

But not now. As crazy as it might seem, Kenyatta had given me something to live for. I had a goal. The idea of checking out before achieving that goal was the furthest thing from my mind.

The psychiatrist left and I tried to sleep. My dreams were all fantasies as I drifted in that twilight between waking and deep slumber; I dreamed of Kenyatta coming to rescue me, taking me back to his house and bathing me like he did that night before the slave auction. Treating my wounds, rubbing me with lotions and scented powders and dressing me in furs. I smiled and wept. Then the phone rang. I snatched it up quickly, hoping it was Kenyatta. I almost said his name until that loathsome voice came whining through the phone. Only this time it was less unctuous, devoid of all threat. It sounded weak. Wounded. It was barely a whisper, but I still recognized it.

"I'm sorry. I'm so sorry. I—we—didn't mean to hurt you. Please...tell him to stop. Okay? Tell him we'll confess. Okay? Tell him...we're so sorry. Just call him off. Don't...don't let him...don't..."

I hung up the phone. There was no question who it was, the same asshole who'd called and threatened me before. Only now, someone had threatened *him*. He sounded completely broken. Terrified. And I knew who had done it. I smiled. I even laughed. Tears of joy ran down my face. Kenyatta still loved me. He was still looking out for me, protecting me. Sleep came easy now. I rolled onto my side and curled into a fetal position. I think I was still smiling when I fell asleep.

"Kitten? You okay?"

He was here.

I woke up and there he was, smiling down at me. I hugged him, pulled him down into the bed with me, and cried on his chest.

"You're here. I thought you weren't coming. I missed you so much."

"I missed you too, Kitten."

I held his hand to my chest, then I looked at it. The knuckles were bruised and swollen. I kissed them and whispered to him. "Thank you."

He smiled back and nodded.

"They are discharging you. They said you didn't suffer any major injuries. Just some minor bruising. No broken bones or anything. They didn't find any evidence of rape either. No vaginal or rectal bruising or tearing. Delia must have gotten to you before they could..."

"Take me home, Daddy. I want to go home," I whined, holding Kenyatta's hand to my face as I wept.

Kenyatta recoiled, snatching his hand away from me. The look on his face was one of shock and disgust. He was looking at me like he'd caught me spreading my legs for another man. I could feel his body tense up. The atmosphere in the room changed. It felt like all the oxygen had been suddenly sucked out. I felt confused. My body trembled.

"Are you quitting? You're giving up?"

"I—"

"Then say the safe word, if you want it to be over."

"Kenyatta, I-I was almost raped!"

That seemed to make him even angrier. I didn't understand. What was going on? Why was he treating me this way? I looked at him, mouth open, unasked questions hovering on my tongue. Delia walked into the room and I looked over at her, my eyes pleaded with her for help, but she would not look at me. As if out of thin air, Kenyatta produced the book, *400 Years of Oppression*. My heart sank, knowing what was about to happen.

"In Africa," he began, "a woman's primary role had been to raise children. Mothers held an honored place in most African societies. On American plantations, this role was perverted with African women being forced into sexual relationships with other slaves, and even with the slavemaster himself, for the purpose of increasing the valuable labor force and satisfying their white master's lascivious desires. The children born of matings with the plantation owners and their female slaves were automatically enslaved. The average female slave gave birth to her first child at nineteen and bore at least one child every two and a half years for as long as she remained fertile. Many of these children were born of rape. Slaves were prohibited by law from defending themselves against physical and sexual abuse and would be subjected to vicious beating by their masters or mistresses for doing so. Rape by their slavemasters and other white men was therefore a constant reality for female slaves, a reality that was ignored by white Christian society."

Delia turned away, looking down at the floor as Kenyatta slammed the book shut, the last word on an argument that had not truly started.

"This is part of my ancestors' reality. All of it! You can't take it? You know what to say if you want out. Say it!"

His eyes were angry. It frightened me, confused me even more.

"Do you want out?"

I dropped my head. My bottom lip trembled and tears flooded from my eyes in an endless deluge of woe.

"No. I'm still in."

Delia handed me my outfit. Stuffing the sundress I'd worn during my ride to the hospital into a plastic bag, she pulled out the latex and leather corset, garters, leggings, and the studded dog collar that had become my uniform on the farm. I wept as I put them back on.

"It's time to go," Kenyatta said and together we left the hospital.

I held onto Kenyatta as he walked down the hall. I buried my head in the space between his chest and his shoulder, squeezing him as if I could hold him there by force and prevent him from leaving me again.

CHAPTER XVI

I returned to my plow and the days and weeks crawled by slowly. Mistress Delia cut me no slack after my ordeal and any laziness on my part was followed by a whipping. On some days, I hoed the fields and planted grape seeds. On others, I picked grapes until the sun set and brought them to the winery by the basketload. Inevitably, I was returned to the plow. My body grew stronger, leaner. A diet of carrots, squash, onions, peppers, okra, yams, tomatoes, leafy greens, corn, black-eyed peas, rice, potatoes, watermelon, grapefruit, apples, and grapes, lots and lots of grapes. Meat of any kind was a rare luxury and usually consisted of very small amounts of pork, chicken and beef from parts of the pig, cow, and chicken I'd never before considered edible. Brains, tongues, intestines, eyes, jawbones, and feet were not uncommon sights in the meager stews I was provided. I didn't know if this nearly vegan diet and the repulsive scraps of meat I was given were yet another chapter in my education on the lives of African slaves or Kenyatta's plan to reshape my thick curvaceous body into one more in line with the modern American female aesthetic. That is to say, skinny. I asked Mistress Delia about it and was surprised when she produced her own copy of the book that had become my bible. It was the first time I'd ever seen her with it. She left the room and returned with it under her arm. The entire time she was speaking, I stared at the book, wondering where she'd gotten it from, if Kenyatta was in the house somewhere, watching me, and had given her the book to read to me. I was so deep in thought that my eyes must have glazed over. Mistress Delia brought me back to attention with a hard slap with the back of her hand that reddened my cheek and made my eyes water.

"Pay attention!"

"Y-yes, Mistress," I stammered, abruptly jarred from my fugue.

"Rice and vegetables were the primary staple of a slave's diet in the South. Meat was a relative luxury and only provided in small portions consisting mainly of the scraps left over from the master's table. These table scraps were the parts of the animal that were considered unfit to be eaten by the slave owners and their families. The legs, feet, jaw, eyes, brain, ribs, tongue, organs, skull, and intestines of butchered animals were given to slaves as a cheap form of nourishment. Better cuts were reserved for the master's table. These undesirable portions were cooked with whatever herbs, spices, and vegetables were common to the area and could be easily scrounged up. Ingenious slaves transformed these animal scraps into palatable meals. Some of the dishes prepared by early slaves, such as pigs intestines (chitterlings) and chicken livers (gizzards) are now considered Southern delicacies."

I nodded and never again complained about my meals. I was a slave and this crap was what slaves ate. I needed to be as ingenious as those early slaves and try to make something tasty out of these horrible scraps of meat, bone, and organs. I began preparing my own meals, experimenting with different herbs and spices until I was able to create recipes for almost every odd piece of animal flesh that was plopped in front of me. That helped make my servitude more bearable.

The police came to the farm once to inquire about the two men who'd assaulted me. Two officers showed up on our doorstep and Mistress Delia called me in from the field to talk with them. I had to take a moment to change my clothes. I was still wearing next to nothing. I joined the two detectives in the family room. There was a tall Asian man in a short-sleeved button down shirt and necktie and a short black guy who reminded me of Danny Glover minus five or six inches in height. They stood as I entered and introduced themselves. I forgot their names seconds after they'd left their lips.

"It seems both men who attacked you were brutally sexually assaulted by an unknown assailant. They have both decided to plead guilty to your attack in exchange for plea bargains. But you don't know anything about that?"

"About what? Who attacked them? No, detective. I don't know who did it. I was in the hospital recovering from the ass-kicking those two bastards gave me."

"And you didn't call a boyfriend, a family member, anyone?" the tall Asian detective said.

"No. You can check my phone records. I didn't call anyone."

"Oh, we will. And if we find anything, we'll be back."

"Detective? Did you ask them who did it? Did they give you a description?"

"We asked them, but they aren't talking. Whoever the guy was who did this, he scared the shit out of them. They won't say a thing."

"What did he...what did their attacker do to them?" I said.

The Danny Glover look-alike spoke up.

"One won't say anything except that he was partially circumcised and beaten half to death. The other was sodomized, first with a bottle that was shattered inside his rectum and then with the business end of a baseball bat. Fucked him up pretty bad. I don't think his bowels will ever function right again. He'll be in adult diapers for the rest of his life."

They left, and I never saw either of them again. The two guys who assaulted me got five years each along with fines and probation. The consensus was they would be out in two with good behavior. I didn't care. I had already gotten my justice. Kenyatta had seen to that.

I was picking grapes the day Mistress Delia walked up to me and announced my emancipation. I wouldn't have believed her if I had not seen Kenyatta behind her in the distance, standing on the porch of the main house. He looked like a mirage to me. I had seen him so many times in my dreams and fantasies, it was hard to convince myself that he was real.

"You're free, girl."

"I-I'm what?" My mind could not comprehend the words coming out of Mistress Delia's mouth. It was like she was speaking some foreign language. What did she mean, I was free? The words didn't make sense.

"Your slavery is over. You're free!"

Mistress Delia looked excited. I was still confused. I wanted to share her excitement. I felt like I should have been happy, but all I felt was deep fear and uncertainty. I no longer knew what freedom meant in this new life of mine. I didn't know what this meant for Kenyatta and I. Was I done? Was I going back to live with Kenyatta? I had underwent only half of my four hundred days of oppression. It couldn't be over, but there was Kenyatta, standing on the porch. I dropped my basket of grapes and ran to him, tripping, cutting my bare feet on rocks and branches, not caring, only wanting to be in his arms again. Tears flew from my eyes and splayed across my cheeks as I raced against the wind. I was sobbing and smiling and laughing. I felt like I was losing my mind. I was so happy. All of my fears and uncertainty left me for a while as I concentrated on Kenyatta, reaching him was my only thought. The world would make sense again, all my pain would be over, if I could just get to that porch, get back to Kenyatta.

Kenyatta smiled when I reached him. I was exhausted, breathing hard. He held out his arms and gathered me up like a bundle of leaves that might be blown away by the slightest breeze if not for his embrace.

"You're coming home."

My legs weakened. I collapsed into his arms, wept against his powerful chest. Kenyatta scooped me up effortlessly and carried me to his car.

The drive home was surreal. The world seemed so different to me now. Everything looked bigger, brighter, louder, faster than I remembered. It was overwhelming, frightening. I clung to Kenyatta's arm, feeling safe against his thick bicep. I closed my eyes and focused on the sound of his breathing, the smell of his cologne, his sweat, his crisp, freshly dry-cleaned clothes. It had been almost two months since I'd been in a car. Not since my trip to and from the hospital. Now I was going home to be with my lover, my Master, my man.

That night, Kenyatta made us dinner. Grilled salmon and shrimp in a creole sauce. Angela was not there. All of her clothes were gone from the closet. No trace of her remained. I had showered, done my hair, even put on makeup for the first time in nearly a year. I was dressed in my old clothes. Everything felt normal again.

"I am so happy right now. It feels so good to be home."

"I missed you," Kenyatta replied, taking my tiny hand in his.

"I was so sad without you. I didn't know what to do. I can't believe it's over."

We sat at the kitchen table eating, holding hands, and smiling at each other. Kenyatta was still smiling at me when he pulled out the book.

"In 1865, following the end of the Civil War, United States President Abraham Lincoln came up with a plan to reconstruct the South. The Freedman's Bureau was created to help thousands of former slaves make a smooth transition into society. The Bureau of Refugees, Freedmen, and Abandoned Lands was a type of early welfare agency providing food, shelter, and medical aid for blacks and whites in need after the Civil War. Its greatest success, however, was in the establishment of 3,000 black schools and the very first black colleges in America. An estimated 200,000 African Americans, who'd been previously denied education by law, were taught how to read and write.

"The Civil Rights Act of 1866 declared all African Americans U.S. citizens, contradicting the 1857 Supreme Court decision in the Dred Scott case which had declared no slave or descendant of a slave could be a U.S. citizen. In 1868, the 14th Amendment was proposed, which declared all people born or naturalized in the U.S. to be citizens, required all states to respect the rights of U.S. citizens regardless of race, creed, or color, provided all citizens with equal protection under the law, and provide all citizens with due process of law. The 15th Amendment was proposed in 1869. It prohibited any state from denying a citizen's right to vote on account of race, color, or previous condition of servitude. The Civil Rights Act of 1875 was the last of the Civil Rights reforms instituted in the Reconstruction era. It guaranteed equal accommodations in public places such as hotels, railroads, theaters, etc. and prohibited courts from excluding African Americans as jurors. Northern soldiers were positioned in the South to enforce the Reconstruction laws and protect the rights of freed slaves as well as to protect them from attacks from Southern whites."

My mouth was hanging open. I had never heard of any of this. If all this were true, then what happened? When did it all go wrong? America seemed to have gotten it right. They had done everything to make sure blacks would get equal rights, a good education, freedom from discrimination. What happened?

Kenyatta continued to read. I hung on every word, not feeling the same dread I normally felt when Kenyatta read from the book. What I felt was excitement, curiosity, and more than a little confusion. How come I didn't know all of this?

"The lives of former slaves improved tremendously during Reconstruction. Many African Americans were overwhelmed with their new rights. They were now full citizens. They could vote, go to school, work for an honest wage, and even run for public office. Hiram Revels was the first African American to be elected to the Senate in Mississippi. African Americans were elected to public office in cities all over the country. There were black sheriffs, black mayors, and a black superintendent of education."

Kenyatta abruptly closed the book, picked up his fork, and resumed his meal, leaving me hanging.

"But what happened? That can't be it! What about Jim Crow?"

Kenyatta smiled, put down his fork, wiped his mouth with his napkin and took my hand again. He looked at me with eyes full of warmth, patience, and understanding. My soul fell into those eyes.

"Let's not ruin the day. There's plenty of time for all of that."

And that's when I knew my education in the black experience in America was not over. This was only a reprieve, the way the 14th and 15th Amendments had been a brief reprieve in the history of black Americans. I tried to enjoy the rest of my meal, but I couldn't. My mind kept drifting back to the book, wondering how Jim Crow laws factored in to what Kenyatta had just read to me and how they were going to factor into our lives in, what I was sure would be, the very near future.

CHAPTER XVII

There were exactly three days of normalcy and bliss. We went shopping together as a couple. Went to eat at an expensive French restaurant downtown. We even got dressed up one night and went to see the San Francisco Ballet do a performance of Bram Stoker's *Dracula*. And, of course, we made love. We made love every day, two or three times a day.

The last day of my reprieve, I was awakened by Kenyatta's tongue against my clitoris and his powerful hands cupping my ass-cheeks like he was holding a large bowl and drinking from it like a savage, greedily lapping up its contents. Judging from his enthusiasm, the bowl formed by his hands contained something singularly sweet and intoxicating. That this "something" was me, made me feel all the more special, loved, desired. His tongue swirled, flicked, and stabbed at my clitoris. I moaned until that was no longer enough to express the ecstasy I felt and then I screamed, exhaling my soul into the ether and inhaling it with the next breath as the little death overcame me. I had my first orgasm of the day mere moments after waking. Then Kenyatta fucked me.

He climbed on top of me and eased himself inside me. I was still tight after so long without him, and it hurt like I haven't hurt since I was a virgin. But Kenyatta was uncharacteristically gentle...at first.

He whispered in my ear as he parted my labia with the head of his cock. I winced and whimpered.

"I love you, Kitten. It's so good to have you back home. I missed your pretty smile. I missed your laugh. And I missed this wonderful pussy."

My entire body quivered at the sound of his voice, a Pavlovian response that resonated to the core of me. Every compliment was like sustenance to the famished, libations to the weary and dehydrated. I gobbled them up, enjoying his words as much as his cock.

Kenyatta's saliva and my own orgasm had left me slippery wet and he slid the rest of his length easily inside of me. The pain took my breath away before giving way to lubricious waves of pleasure as Kenyatta began to slowly grind and thrust, moving his hips in slow semi-circles as his cock seemed to touch my spine. He grabbed my full hips, using them for leverage, pulling me off the mattress to meet each thrust as his lovemaking became less gentle.

He tossed both of my legs over his shoulders, maintaining eye contact as he pounded himself inside of me, brutalizing my pussy. I pinched his nipples, trying to make him cum before he broke me, but finding my own flesh responding to his rough lovemaking with shocks of pleasure. An unexpected orgasm took hold of me as Kenyatta whipped his head back and roared. His body tensed as he shot his seed deep inside me. My vagina felt bruised and swollen. My clitoris felt like it had been used as a speed bag, nevertheless, I came hard. My body bucked and convulsed with the force of the sudden climax. Kenyatta was still staring into my eyes, watching me cum. When I lay still, spent and exhausted, he smiled at me.

"I love you, Kitten."

"I love you too, Kenyatta."

That day we went window shopping at a jewelry store. We picked out a wedding ring to match the engagement ring that was still in Kenyatta's possession. We went to a bridal shop and I tried on gowns. I was beaming while the sales women buzzed around me, telling me how lovely I looked in this dress or that dress and what a lovely couple we made. I could not have imagined a more perfect day. Everything I had gone through the last 300 days seemed like a memory. Then we went home and reality put its foot firmly in my naive ass.

We had just walked in when I noticed my bags were packed and sitting by the door. The next thing I noticed was Angela reclining on the couch with an Indian woman in a beautiful red and gold saree whom I'd never seen before. I assumed the woman was Angela's new girlfriend. But that didn't explain why all of my shit was packed.

"Hi, Angela. What's going on?" I turned to Kenyatta and gestured toward my packed bags. "What's going on?"

This time, when Kenyatta opened the book, I knew I wouldn't like what he was about to read me.

"Only ten years after the 14th and 15th Amendments were passed, granting freed slaves full citizenship and equal rights, federal troops withdrew from the South, returning it to local white rule. The Republican Party, then the champion of Reconstruction and Freedmen's rights, had lost their hold on the reins of national power. From the late 1870s, Southern state legislatures, no longer controlled by carpetbaggers and freedmen, passed laws requiring the separation of whites from "persons of color" in public transportation and schools. Anyone strongly suspected of black ancestry was for this purpose a "person of color." Parks, cemeteries, theaters, and restaurants were segregated to prevent any contact between blacks and whites as societal equals. In 1890, despite 16 black members holding office at that time and voting on the issue, the Louisiana General Assembly passed a law to prevent black and white people from riding together on railroads. A case challenging the law, Plessy v. Ferguson, reached the U.S. Supreme Court in 1896. The law, along with similar laws on the state and local level, was codified by the Supreme Court ruling that public facilities for blacks and whites could be "separate but equal." The immediate effect of the ruling was that, throughout the South, they had to be separate. Southern states began to limit voting rights to those who owned property or could read well, to those whose grandfathers had been able to vote, to those with "good characters," to those who paid poll taxes, or could pass any number of tests not required of white voters. In 1896, Louisiana had 130,334 registered black voters.

Eight years later, only 1,342—1 percent—could pass the state's new rules.

"These new laws separating blacks from whites were known as "Jim Crow Laws," a derogatory epithet for blacks that came from a minstrel routine (*Jump Jim Crow*) performed beginning in 1828 by its author, Thomas Dartmouth ("Daddy") Rice, along with many imitators. Jim Crow laws spread throughout the South and quickly became a way of life. In South Carolina, many businesses would not allow black and white employees to work in the same room, enter through the same door, or even gaze out of the same window. Many industries wouldn't hire blacks at all. Unions passed rules explicitly excluding black workers from joining, which then excluded them from union jobs, beginning a cycle of chronic unemployment and economic disenfranchisement, which continues to this day.

"In Richmond, blacks could not live on the same street as whites. By 1914, Texas had six entire towns that excluded black residents. In Mobile, Alabama, blacks could not leave their homes after 10 p.m. "Whites Only" or "Colored" signs became common sights throughout the South, separating pools, bathrooms, restaurants, theaters, ticket windows, drinking fountains, even entrances and exits. There were separate parks, phone booths, prisons, hospitals, orphanages, churches, schools, and colleges. Black and white students had to use separate sets of textbooks. Some jurisdictions wouldn't even allow the books to be stored together. Courts kept separate bibles for swearing in a witness: one for black witnesses and one for whites.

"States in the North did not go unaffected by Jim Crow. Discrimination spread like a cancer. Unwritten rules barred blacks from white jobs in New York and kept them out of white stores in Los Angeles. In 1915, the Ku Klux Klan was revived and lynchings and cross-burnings 'punished' blacks who disobeyed Jim Crow laws, using the fear of violence to keep blacks 'in their place.'"

I shook my head. Again, joy was replaced by pain, elation with disappointment. Hours ago we were picking out wedding rings and now my life, my world, was about to be turned upside down again,

"This is Shakeela Geeti. She is a Mehndi artist."

"Mehndi?"

"A tattooist. She does henna tattoos."

"Henna tattoos?"

I looked at the woman in the colorful saree. Then at Angela who smiled at me. None of the hostility she'd shown to me when we first met, before we'd fucked, was reflected in her expression. What I saw there was something new, something worse...pity.

"Who's getting the tattoo?"

Kenyatta smiled. It was a horrible sight. There was nothing warm in the expression. For the first time I recognized a hint of mischief and malevolence. He was getting off on this.

"You are. On your face."

"My face? Why?"

"How else will you learn about discrimination? You want to know what it's like for black people to walk into a job interview, apply for a bank loan, walk into a department store, and be judged, dismissed, despised the minute they look at your face? Your face will make you a second-class citizen just like we were for seventy years following the Emancipation Proclamation, free but not free, emancipated but still oppressed. Everywhere you go, people will take one look at you and attach half a dozen negative stereotypes to you."

I shook my head. Tears wept from my eyes.

"Come on, Kenyatta. No. I-I can't do that."

The whips. The chains. The hard labor. The terrible food. The pain. I could endure it all again if I needed to, but going out in public to be looked down upon, ridiculed, rejected. It was too much. It had only been a few days since I was given my freedom and now this new humiliation… It was too much.

"You want to quit?"

"No...but...not this. Come on, Kenyatta. This is too much. I can't do it."

"You know what to say if you want it to end."

I looked at him, at Angela, at the Indian woman, and the thought crossed my mind. The word crossed my mind.

"Why are my bags packed?"

"You're free. You can't live in the Master's house anymore. You have to get a job and find your own apartment."

I dropped my head and shook it in disbelief.

"With a fucking tattoo on my face?" I practically screamed the words at him. I was hysterical. This was just too much.

Kenyatta was still smiling when he answered.

"Yes. With a fucking tattoo on your face. It isn't permanent. It'll fade away in two or three weeks. I promise."

I felt like I was going to throw up. Everything we'd done so far had been private, between him and I and other people in the BDSM scene. People who would understand. Going out in public like this was something I hadn't counted on. I tried to imagine walking into a job interview with my face covered in tattoos. There was no way. How would I support myself?

As if in response to my unspoken question, Kenyatta read from the book. I wanted to snatch it out of his hands and rip it to shreds.

"The 13th Amendment meant freedom for four million African-American slaves. However, faced with overwhelming discrimination, the majority of them soon found themselves poor and unemployed. For African Americans, finding employment in Northern cities was a difficult and sometimes impossible task. Discriminatory labor practices, demanded by European immigrants, often denied African Americans skilled jobs. Southern migrants were particularly disadvantaged since they were more likely than Northern-born blacks to have job skills. Many freed slaves were compelled to abandon their trades due to unrelenting racial prejudice and take menial, low-paying, unskilled jobs. Philadelphia employment records reveal that during this period, less than two-thirds of [black workers] who had trades followed them.

"In New York City, officials reneged on their promise to 'issue licenses to all regardless of race' and buckled under pressure from white workers to exclude African Americans from jobs requiring special permits. One foreign visitor reported seeing almost no black skilled workers in the North. The few exceptions were 'one or two employed as printers, one blacksmith and one shoemaker.' African Americans found it almost impossible to obtain licenses, denying them important opportunities to become small businessmen and elevate their economic status. Many former slaves were forced to go back to the plantations from which they were freed and work for their former owners in agricultural jobs for very little compensation.

"In an attempt to earn enough to avoid starvation, entire families would contract with a landowner to cultivate the land for subsistence wages or a share of the crop. Often their white employers continued to treat them as slaves and attempted to control their comings and goings, limit or prohibit visitors, and dictate their behavior. The struggle between former slaves trying, often unsuccessfully, to differentiate their employment from their previous servitude and former slaveholders, used to having total control over their workers, led to postwar workplaces that were tense, and often violent. Many former slaves did not receive the wages promised in their labor contracts, while others never found employment at all and were reduced to begging on the streets, crime, and prostitution."

He closed the book and glared at me.

"Do you think you'll have it any harder than those freed slaves?"

"No."

"So, what's it going to be? Are you out or in?"

Again, I looked at Shakeela, at Angela, and then back at Kenyatta who was tapping his foot impatiently. I let out a long sigh and wiped the tears from my eyes.

"I'm in."

Kenyatta took my hand and led me to a seat opposite Shakeela.

"Relax," she cooed as she cupped my face in two incredibly smooth soft hands. She turned my face left then right. Then picked up a little squirt bottle filled with a dark paste. It took her two hours to draw the design on my face and another six hours for it to set up, during which she would occasionally sprinkle lemon and water or eucalyptus oil on the paste to keep it moist.

I wasn't allowed to look at my face in the mirror until the tattoo had properly cured. I imagined that Kenyatta was afraid I would quit and wash it all off before it could set up. When it was finally ready, I could tell from the expression on Angela's face, eyes wide, brow furrowed, lips pulled back away from her teeth in a grim rictus, that Kenyatta had done something awful to me. He led me to the bathroom and watched as I got my first glimpse of the abomination she'd drawn on my face. It was all I could do to keep from screaming.

"No. No! What the hell did you do to me?"

On my forehead, cheeks, chin, nose, beneath my eyes, even my eyelids, were flowers, paisleys, leaves and various lines and squiggles forming geometrical patterns in a dark rusty red. But what made me want to scream was what I saw in those patterns, in the lines and squiggles...words. They weren't immediately apparent, hidden in the highly stylized calligraphy, amidst the floral patterns and designs, hateful, despicable words. "Lazy." "Stupid." "Violent." "Thief." "Slut." "Liar." "Criminal." "Drug Dealer." "Gang Banger." "Addict." The closer I looked, the clearer and more prominent the words became. I had been labeled with every negative stereotype with which society had labeled black Americans. It stained my skin like the mark of Cain and it would remain there for weeks.

"The first thing black children all over America, for almost four centuries, learned was to hate their own skin, their own faces. That is part of the experience. Your disgust when you look in the mirror, seeing that you don't look anything like the beautiful people on TV, that's part of it. The other part will be the suspicion, hatred, disgust, and distrust others will show you because of your skin. That's how you'll really know what it's like."

Kenyatta paid the Indian woman and showed her to the door. Then he showed me to the door as well.

"I'll give you twenty-four hours to find a job and an apartment. Then you've got to go."

He shoved me gently onto the porch, kissed my forehead, rubbed, squeezed, then smacked my ample buttocks, and slammed the door behind me. I stood there on the porch, weeping for moments that felt like hours, before taking a deep breath and once again wiping the tears from my eyes. I had to at least try.

Chapter XVIII

Catching a taxi was my first difficulty. I walked to the nearest convenience store, eyes from passing pedestrians followed me. Children giggled and pointed. An old white lady in a red motorized scooter sneered at me in disgust and shook her head. I felt thoroughly wretched. This was worse than the box in the basement.

The teenaged convenience store clerk looked up from his computer gamer magazine long enough to glare at me, smirk, tsk, and shake his head, before immediately reaching for his smartphone, presumably to text his buddies about the tattooed freak who'd just walked into his store. Ironic and a bit hypocritical of him considering the sleeve of dragons, zombies, and sexy devil chicks that ran up his left arm. But, of course, there were fathoms between the sort of antisocial behavior that led one to tattoo a devil in a black bikini riding a Chinese dragon on their arm and the type of insanity that led a woman to allow a man to tattoo insults all over her face.

"Hi...uh...do you know the best place around here to catch a cab?"

"Cool tattoo."

I blushed and looked away, not certain if he was fucking with me or not.

"Uh...thanks...um..."

"Taxi, right? They drive by occasionally, but you'd have better luck calling one. I'll call one for you."

He took out his smartphone, removed a yellow business card from somewhere behind the counter, and quickly dialed the number. I looked around the store at the rows of unhealthy snacks: chips, candies, packaged cupcakes and cookies, so-called energy and "nutrition" bars, all packed with enough preservatives to ensure they'd endure a generation. Juxtaposed with stationary, paper goods, toiletries, a few odd supermarket items like bread, cake mix, pet food, soup, beans, ravioli and other canned goods. Another aisle contained automotive supplies, aspirin, allergy and sinus medications and various other pharmaceuticals. It had never occurred to me before how weird convenience stores were.

"They said they'll be here in twenty minutes," the kid behind the counter said.

"Thanks."

Twenty minutes. That meant I'd be stuck here with nothing to do but wander the aisles and wait for the next person to come in and gawk at me. It didn't take long for the first customers to arrive. A group of Filipino teenagers with their pants sagging down below their waists so their multicolored boxers were visible, wearing 49ers jerseys, walked in. They wore practiced sneers of contempt that became genuine only when they looked at me. One of them laughed. I was mortified.

"Check out the tattooed chick," one of them whispered.

"That's crazy, yo!"

I left the store snatching a free weekly newspaper off a stand by the front door on my way out. This time I shielded my face as I walked. My embarrassment was etched into my skin deeper than the tattoo ink. I walked to the corner and sat down on a bench, trying to read the classified ads through a veil of tears.

There were ads for teachers, tutors, nannies, all jobs I would have been qualified for, but imagining myself walking into an interview with "Slut," "Thief," "Addict," and "Drug Dealer" tattooed on my face made me skip those jobs. As I circled a cocktail waitress job and prepared to call, I wondered if black people did the same thing, skipping jobs they were qualified for out of fear of rejection. Then I reconsidered. I picked the highest paying job listed, an English teacher at a private girls' school, and used my smartphone to email them my resume. I sent it to seven other places, including a couple in Berkeley advertising for a live-in nanny. That would've solved both of my most immediate problems: money and shelter. I decided to give them a call. I took a deep breath, wiped the last remnants of tears from my eyes, and dialed the number.

"Hello?" said a woman with a raspy voice as if she'd been smoking a pack-a-day since birth and chasing it with moonshine.

"Hi, My name is Natasha Talusa. I'm calling about your ad for a live-in nanny. Is the position still available?"

"Yes. Yes. We are conducting interviews today. What time can you come by?"

"I'll be coming on BART so it will take me at least an hour."

"Okay. That's fine. I don't have any other appointments today. Hopefully you'll be the fit we're looking for. Do you have any experience?"

"I taught seventh grade English for five years, and I have a degree in childhood education."

"Sounds good. I can't wait to meet you."

I allowed myself to be hopeful as I rode the BART across the bay into Oakland and all the way to Berkeley. I ignored the stares and snickers and instead concentrated on what I would say to my prospective employer. I'd have to be damned charming to make up for my appearance.

The BART train was crowded, as usual. This allowed me to hide among the crush of humanity. The scowls of disgust were limited to those in my immediate vicinity, but the more the crowd thinned as we headed into Berkeley, the more those scowls multiplied, shaking my nerves and causing me to question my resolve. Perhaps I should have stuck to cocktail waitress jobs or maybe even a truck stop waitress.

"Who would write 'slut' or their forehead? That's what it says isn't it?" said a college student of mixed heritage. One of those unusual combinations of race that only Berkeley produced; black, Samoan, Filipino, and Irish or something similar. He had cinnamon colored skin, slanted hazel eyes, a wide nose, thick lips, and a thick wooly Afro. His friends, three of whom shared his exotic features, but were probably not related, all snickered. One pointed at me. I moved into the next car with them laughing at my back as I exited. I wiped tears from my eyes. This was probably the most liberal city in America. If I was getting ridiculed here, there was little hope for me.

The next car was practically empty, and I sat alone at the back, waiting for the ride to end. I called two more job listings in the Berkeley area while I was on the train. One was for a daycare provider at the University and the other was for a tutor. Finally, the train pulled to a stop at Berkeley station. I stood and walked out of the car as others rushed on. A woman with close-cropped hair, a black leather motorcycle jacket and "SAN FRANCISCO" tattooed on her neck in large gothic lettering smiled at me and said: "Cool tattoo!" Then an expression of perplexity crossed her face as she continued staring at the designs painted onto my skin, no doubt seeing the words for the first time. I thanked her and hurried past.

I hailed a taxi, gave the man the address and sank into the back seat, hiding my face and trying to avoid eye contact with the driver or do anything else that might encourage conversation. It was a wasted effort.

"What's that on your face?" the driver said. He was a young Nigerian man with a thick accent. I didn't look up to read his name badge on the dashboard of his car. I didn't want to give him a better view of my face.

He was staring at me in the rearview mirror. I looked away.

"Please keep your eyes on the road," I responded, and we drove the rest of the way in silence.

The house was in the Berkeley Hills, one of the most expensive neighborhoods in the Bay Area, comparable to Pacific Heights in San Francisco or "Specific Whites" as Kenyatta called it. The taxi driver dropped me off in front of a huge Victorian with large columns and a front porch the size of my last apartment. I approached the porch on shaky legs.

The doorbell sounded like a gong. All the moisture on my body seemed to have doubled as I waited for someone to answer. The door swung wide and an elegant woman in her forties wearing a Chanel pants suit, stood in the doorway, smiling wide in welcome. Her smile quickly fell from her face and all the joy left her eyes.

"May I help you?"

"Hi, I'm Natasha Talusa. I called about the position."

I held out my hand and the woman looked at it like it was something that had floated up from a toilet.

"I'm sorry, the position has been filled," she said and closed the door, leaving me standing on the front porch with my hand still outstretched, the fake smile still on my face. I turned and walked off the porch, sobbing. I had no idea what I was going to do.

I hit the two other jobs with similar results. At the university, the woman conducting the interview started laughing when she saw me.

"You've got to be kidding me? Did someone put you up to this?"

"No ma'am I—"

"This is a joke, right? Who put you up to this? One of the girls?"

"No ma'am. I have a degree in childhood education. I have an English degree. I worked for the San Francisco school district for five years—"

"Stop. Let me stop you right there. Sweetie, I cannot hire a woman with tattoos all over her face, no matter how many degrees you have. I'm sorry, but there's just no way you can teach children with 'Thief,' 'Addict,' 'Criminal,' and...does that say 'Slut'? There's just no way."

"I understand. Thank you for your time."

I walked out feeling lower than I ever had at any other time in the experiment. The obstacle Kenyatta had set before me this time was impossible. I rode the BART train back home in tears. What the hell was I going to do? Kenyatta wanted me out of the house in twenty-four hours.

I made it back to Kenyatta's home ten hours after I left that morning. Kenyatta was there waiting for me, as was Angela.

"How did it go?"

"This is impossible! No one will hire me like this. I can't get a job. So how am I supposed to get an apartment?"

Kenyatta leaned forward and stroked my hair then put a hand on my cheek.

"Then do what tens of thousands of freed slaves did before you. Go back to the plantation."

CHAPTER XIX

The next morning, I decided to try it again. This time I lowered my expectations. I could take a waitressing job now and could always continue looking for a higher paying job that utilized my education while I was working.

I sat at the kitchen table with Kenyatta and Angela. I had slept in the shed again last night, once more relegated to slave quarters while Angela enjoyed all the comforts of home. Following my job-hunting ordeal, this second insult, and the idea that Kenyatta may have been fucking her was almost too much to take. I was quiet as I ate my eggs and bacon, seething in silent rage. Kenyatta tried again and again to draw me into a conversation.

"This is your last day. What did you decide to do? Are you going back to the plantation or are you going to try finding a job again?"

I didn't answer, didn't even look up from the plate.

"Did you hear me?"

I nodded.

"Well?"

"I'm not going back." I still did not look at him.

"Well, good luck finding an apartment."

I ignored the comment and kept eating. I heard Angela clear her throat to get Kenyatta's attention. Out of the corner of my eye I saw her shake her head, trying to signal Kenyatta to back off. She could clearly sense that I was about to lose it.

"Well, I'm off to work. Goodbye, Kitten."

I didn't respond. Kenyatta reached out and grabbed my plate, pulling it away from me. With his other hand he seized my jaw and tilted my head up, trying to force me to look at him. I kept my eyes averted.

"I said, Goodbye! Look at me!"

I looked at him with all the hate I could muster. I was angry, and I wanted him to know that, but he would also know I didn't hate him. My love was so much stronger than any anger I felt toward him. I met his eyes.

"It's almost over, Kitten. Hang in there. You've been through too much to let this break you."

And he was right of course. I had been through too much. This shouldn't have been that bad after all I'd suffered, but it was precisely because I'd suffered so much that this last part was so difficult. The way that woman looked at me when she told me there was no job and closed the door in my face. How that woman had bluntly told me she'd never hire a woman with a tattoo on her face. Kenyatta had done well. If this is how blacks felt, the prejudice they encountered when they were trying to find a job to feed themselves and their families, it was no wonder so many turned to crime or languished on public assistance. This was completely demoralizing.

"You still want to be my wife?" Kenyatta said.

All the anger in me diminished instantly at the prospect.

"Y-yes, of course. Of-of course I do," I said. An unexpected tear raced from my eye and Kenyatta leaned in and kissed it away. He kissed both eyelids, kissed my forehead, then planted one, long, soulful kiss on my lips that made my knees weak.

"Good luck today, Kitten. I love you."

"I love you too, Kenyatta," I replied.

I felt better, more resolved. As Kenyatta walked out the door, I was already preparing myself to do battle in the job market. Then Angela spoke up and ruined everything.

"You're a fool, you know that right?"

"Angela, don't." I held up a hand to silence her.

"He's playing you. You know you're not the first white woman he's done this to?"

I looked at her in shock.

"He didn't tell you? You're not the first, but you have come the farthest. Most quit in the box. He's had to get real creative to keep challenging you. He never expected you to make it this far."

I shook my head.

"I don't believe you."

But what she was saying made sense. Why would I have been the first? Did I think I was the first white woman he'd ever dated? Did I think I was the first one he'd ever loved?

"Did he ever tell you about the first white woman he ever fell in love with? What he did to her family?"

I shook my head. I didn't think I wanted to hear this.

"She told him she couldn't see him because her parents were prejudice, so Kenyatta took a knife, went to her house, and killed them both. He stabbed the girl's mother about twenty times and her father more than fifty. He slit the man's throat so deep he almost decapitated him. He was only fourteen so he was tried as a juvenile and declared insane. They put him in a mental institution until he was an adult. On his twenty-first birthday, he was released and his juvenile record was sealed. He killed two people and walked out of there with a clean record."

My hands shook as I stood up and began clearing the breakfast dishes. I didn't know what to think. How could Kenyatta have killed someone? It didn't make sense. But the real problem was that it made too much sense. It answered too many questions.

I slammed the dishes down in the sink, shattering them.

"Why the fuck are you telling me this now? Why didn't you say something before?"

Angela stood up and tried to put her arms around me. I pushed her away.

"Why now? Answer me!"

"Because you might make it. I never thought you would before, but you might make it. And marrying him would be the biggest mistake of your life. Kenyatta doesn't love you. He doesn't know how to love anyone. All he's got inside him is hate. He wants everyone, every white person, to feel the pain he felt when he was rejected at fourteen. That's what he's in this for, and it won't stop when this is over. It won't stop when you get a ring on your finger. You need to think about this, girl."

And I did. I thought about it while I walked to the bus stop. I thought about it as I rode the bus to the BART train. I thought about it as I took BART to Market Street and even while I walked up Market to my first job interview. It was all I could think about. Had all this been for nothing? Was Angela just saying all that because she wanted him to herself? But that didn't make sense. Angela was a lesbian. That could have been bullshit though. She was definitely bi, but just because she liked pussy didn't mean she didn't also love dick.

The interview was for a job as a waitress at a diner on Market and Church Street. I tilted my head back, lifted my chin, and marched in. The diner was designed to look like the dining car of an old train. Being in San Francisco, there was every possibility that it had once been. It was green and black with little green shades on the windows with gold tassels. Every seat was filled and the waitresses looked harried but competent as they hurried up and down the aisles taking and delivering food orders. I could easily imagine myself among them. It would actually be a relief to have a job, for once, that ended when you clocked out. No tests or papers to grade or assignments to plan. No stressing over some complicated lesson plan or student issue. Just take the order and bring the food. No thought involved. It would be a relief.

I walked up to the cash register and put on my brightest smile.

"Hi. I'm here to apply for the waitress position."

The woman behind the counter had thick blonde curls and bright red lipstick. She dressed in a tight cream-colored cashmere sweater and a black poodle skirt with a red kitten on it, like she stepped off the set of *Happy Days*. But she was much too young to have ever seen the show, except perhaps in reruns. There was some odd combination of smile and frown on her face that was supposed to be sexy, judging from the way she stood with one hand on her hip, breasts thrust out prominently, twirling her gum around her finger and winking at customers as they walked in.

"Um, okay. Have you ever waitressed before?" she said, glancing my way only long enough to pass me an application before she resumed smiling and winking at customers. She even flirted with the gay couples.

"No...um...not really."

She turned and looked at me, really looked at me, for the first time.

"Is that permanent?" she said, gesturing toward my face, with a dismissive flip of the wrist. I wanted to grab her by the hair and slam her face into the cash register. Instead, I willed myself to hold that fake smile on my face like it was chained to me.

"No. It only lasts two or three weeks."

She looked me up and down then turned to blow a kiss at an old man I assumed was a regular. He returned the gesture, beaming from ear to ear.

"We might still be hiring in three weeks," she said, without ever turning back to look at me. I stood there for nearly a full minute, during which she never looked at me again. Finally, I walked out of the little diner, refusing to cry, determined not to give up. I caught a bus to Haight Street and walked down to the Lower Haight district where there were quirky little shops and bars that were used to people with odd tattoos and piercings.

There was a bar called The Mad Wolf that had advertised for a cocktail waitress. It was right in the middle of the block. The kind of bar with saloon doors, pool tables, dart boards, and a sparse smattering of lonely drunks, having their first drink of the day when most people were still digesting their Froot Loops.

I walked up to the bar. The guy behind it was a big, six-foot, urban redneck/punk in a black cowboy hat, a black Sex Pistols t-shirt with the sleeves torn off, black jeans, and black combat boots with spurs on them. He had gray hair and crow's feet at the corners of his eyes and lips. He was old enough to have seen Sid Vicious live.

"What's up?"

"I'm here about the cocktail waitress job?"

"What's the tattoo for?"

"It's a long story."

He leaned over the bar and locked eyes with me.

"If you want to work here, I think I need to hear it."

"Basically, my boyfriend wanted me to see if I could get a job looking like this."

His eyes remained fixed on me, and his expression was deadpan. I felt so uncomfortable under his gaze that I almost turned and left.

"Ever worked in a bar before?" he said finally.

"No. I was a schoolteacher. I taught seventh grade English."

"But you couldn't teach kids with 'Slut' and 'Liar' tattooed on your face, so you're slumming at a bar, hoping my standards are low enough to hire you?"

I smiled and nodded.

"I guess so."

"Well. You're in luck. My standards are just that low. Welcome to the Mad Wolf!"

He spread his arms wide and gestured around the nearly empty bar.

"Thanks!" I said, a little too energetically.

"It pays nine dollars plus tips. Most girls make a hundred a night in tips. Two hundred on the busy nights. That okay?"

"That sounds perfect."

I reached across the bar and shook his hand then turned to leave, but he didn't let go.

"You in a hurry? Let me show you around the bar."

He stroked my arm with his other hand and I quickly snatched my hand away.

"I...um...I—"

He smiled a wide predatory smile.

"Let me show you where we keep all the kegs and the cases of beer." He leaned close enough for me to smell the marijuana and beer on his breath. "We've got a bed back there."

"No. I don't think so," I said.

"Come on. Why not? I told you I'd hire you."

"So I'm supposed to fuck you for a job?"

He sneered at me.

"You're the whore with 'Slut' tattooed on your forehead," he said.

"Fuck you!" I yelled. My voice echoed in the near empty bar. A few of the drunks laughed. The others barely looked up from their drinks.

"Fucking asshole!" I flipped him the bird over my shoulder as I stormed out.

"You're fired!" he yelled back and then I heard him laugh. His laughter was worse than any insult he could have hurled at me. I wanted to crawl in a hole and die.

I stormed out of the bar. That was it. The last straw. Fuck this. I walked back to the bus stop. I was done. I had a decision to make. I could either go back to the plantation, as Kenyatta suggested, or I could say fuck the whole thing, as Angela suggested.

An hour later, when I walked up the steps of Kenyatta's home and opened the front door, I was still undecided. It was the sound of the headboard smacking the wall, the moans and screams coming from Kenyatta's bedroom, that made up my mind.

CHAPTER XX

He was fucking her. I walked in and caught him, fucking his ex-wife. Fucking her hard and angry. Crushing her into the mattress with each stroke. His ass was poised in the air, preparing for the down stroke, that beautiful, muscular ass I loved so much, poised there. Her legs tossed over his shoulders, her moans of pain and pleasure echoing from everywhere.

He had been fucking her all along. I don't know why I was surprised. I would have had to be a fool to think he wasn't. But, I had been that fool. Even as I was lying on a bed of straw in the backyard, as I was being whipped and almost raped at Mistress Delia's farm, pulling a plow and picking grapes. As I was being humiliated day after day, walking the streets with this damned tattoo on my face, I had believed every second that there would be a happily-ever-after for Kenyatta and I. I had believed that he would love me and protect me and be all those things a man was supposed to be according to the romance novels and romantic comedies.

Angela spotted me first and the look of guilt on her face confirmed everything.

"Oh, shit!"

She pushed Kenyatta off her and pulled the sheets up to her chin in some ridiculous show of false modesty. I had fucked this woman. I licked her pussy and she licked mine. What did she think she was hiding that I had not already seen? But she wasn't hiding her body, she was holding up a shield, protecting herself with the only thing she had, a thin sheet. Kenyatta, however, was unfazed. He stood, naked, cock still hard and bobbing in the air like a divining rod. He held out his arms for me.

"Come join us."

That's when I found my voice.

"NIGGERRRRRRRR!" I screamed it loud and long. Then I screamed it again.

I picked up whatever I could find off the dresser and threw it at him as I repeated it over and over again. "NIGGER! NIGGER! NIGGEEEEEEERRRRRR!"

Kenyatta rushed across the room, raised his hand, and slapped me to the floor. He didn't slap me as a master slapping his willing slave. There was nothing safe or sane about it. Perhaps there never had been. I had been slapped like this by men before. There was anger in his eyes and in his heart. It hurt me more than anything else I'd endured during those long arduous months of servitude. I turned and walked out, Kenyatta chased behind me, apologizing, begging me to stay. I guess the safe word didn't matter anymore.

"Okay! Okay! Wait! Forget about the experiment. It's over. I don't care about the safe word. I'll marry you, okay? I'll marry you!"

He was standing there in the doorway as I walked out onto the porch, down the front steps and down the walkway toward my car. He was naked, beautiful, but somehow pathetic, diminished, and not merely because his cock had shriveled. I could see him now clearly for what he was, a sad, lonely, angry man who was full of self-loathing.

His ancestors had been through horrors and atrocities that most people could scarcely imagine, let alone survive. From the Trans-Atlantic slave trade and Jim Crow, through the civil rights movement, right up to the insidious institutionalized racism that holds so many of his people in economic dungeons to this day. Black people in America have suffered what no race of people should have ever had to endure, but *he* hadn't. Kenyatta had never been a slave. He had never been through segregation. He was handsome, successful, and should have been happy. But he would never be, because he clearly hated himself. I pitied him now, and I could never marry him.

"Goodbye, Kenyatta."

I turned my back, shaking my head, as the tears began to flow. I kept my head held high as I strode down that walkway to the sidewalk, sobbing openly, heartbroken. I felt hollow inside, shattered and gutted. But I was me again. I'd been here before. I was no one's slave anymore. I was no one's second-class citizen. The tattoo would fade. I'd get a job, and my life would resume. I'd come back from heartache after heartache and I would come back from this one. What Kenyatta put me through, would always be a part of me. Like it or not, he had taught me a lot about race and racism. Things I would never forget. He'd literally scarred these lessons into my flesh. Perhaps I owed him for that...but fuck him.

I didn't know where my car keys were. Kenyatta had taken them from me when we first began this sadistic game. I didn't care. I kept walking past my car, down the street, to the nearest bus stop. I sat there, seesawing from relief, to anger, to overwhelming sadness. I didn't know what I should do next, then I cautiously probed my cheek with my fingertips. It was swollen and still felt warm to the touch from where Kenyatta had slapped me. My lip was swollen as well and I could taste blood in my mouth. I sighed deeply, pulled out my cell phone, and called 911.

EPILOGUE

⌐⌐

I sat down at an outdoor café in South Beach, sipping a mimosa and waiting on a shrimp cocktail. The tattoo had faded away months ago. I was back working for the school district after cutting my hiatus short. My life was almost back to normal.

I pressed charges against Kenyatta for slapping me and took out a restraining order against him. Angela called me a few times to beg me to reconsider. She even threatened me on more than one occasion until I recorded one of her more hostile phone calls and had her arrested for making terrorist threats. That was four months ago, and I haven't heard from either of them since.

The waitress brought my shrimp cocktail, and I made a mental note to leave her a big tip. I took another sip of my mimosa and was just about to dig into the shrimp cocktail, when a familiar silhouette caught my attention. He was across the street at a used bookstore. He wore a white shirt and a red tie with the sleeves rolled up like a politician on the campaign trail. There was a woman on his arm, a tall blonde with big tits, wide hips, and a big round ass. Kenyatta's type. He reached over and patted the woman on her ass. I could hear her giggle from across the street.

When I saw the collar around her neck, the same one I had worn, I felt a twinge of jealousy. Then I spotted the book in his hand. I couldn't read the title from where I was, but I didn't need to. I had seen it so many times before. When he opened it and began to read from it to the tall blonde, a chill raised over my skin. He was doing it again. He had found another victim for his twisted mind games, another fool.

I reached into my wallet and pulled out two twenties to cover the bill, then I stood and began walking across the street. I reached into my purse one more time. Living alone in the city was scary sometimes. I had long ago taken to carrying protection. I felt the familiar weight of it in my hand as I approached the two of them. I had been submissive for far too long. It was time to end the game for real. And this time, there would be no safe word.

ACKNOWLEDGEMENTS

Special thanks to R.J. Cavender and Marc Ciccarone for having faith in this project. Thanks to Monica O'Rourke for her invaluable editing advice. Tod Clark for his keen eye for the little things. And Christie White for the inspiration.

ABOUT THE AUTHOR

Wrath James White is a former World Class Heavyweight Kickboxer, a professional Kickboxing and Mixed Martial Arts trainer, distance runner, performance artist, and former street brawler, who is now known for creating some of the most disturbing works of fiction in print.

Wrath is the author of *The Resurrectionist, Succulent Prey, Yaccub's Curse, Sacrifice, Pure Hate,* and *Prey Drive* (*Succulent Prey Part II*). He is also the author of *Voracious, To The Death, Skinzz, The Reaper, Like Porno For Psychos, Everyone Dies Famous In A Small Town, The Book Of A Thousand Sins, His Pain* and *Population Zero*. He is the co-author of *Teratologist* co-written with the king of extreme horror, Edward Lee, *Orgy Of Souls* co-written with Maurice Broaddus, *The Killings* and *Hero* co-written with J.F. Gonzalez, and *Poisoning Eros I* and *II* co-written with Monica J. O'Rourke.

DREW STEPEK

"Stepek is masterful in enabling the reader to actually feel sorrow and empathy for a few of the characters and to see the human in the monsters and the monster in the humans. 3.5 skulls out of 4."

~ Fangoria Magazine

"Combining the slick Hollywood decadence of a Bret Easton Ellis novel and the drug-addled realism of Irvine Welsh's *Trainspotting*, author Drew Stepek gleefully takes the piss out of the staid troupes of the genre..."

~ *Rue Morgue Magazine*

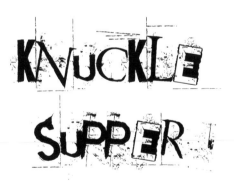

ISBN-13: 978-0984978281
Available at www.bloodboundbooks.net, your local bookstore or favorite webstore. Also in e-book formats!

D.O.A. II – EXTREME HORROR ANTHOLOGY

"Make sure your health insurance covers psychiatric counseling before reading this book, because you're gonna need it. The experience of this collection may be likened to getting run over by a 666-car locomotive engineered by Lucifer. This is the cream of grotesquerie's crop, a Whitman's Sampler of the heinous, and an absolutely gut-wrenching celebration of the furthest extremities of the scatological, the taboo, the unconscionable, and the blasphemous."

~ Edward Lee, author of *The Haunter of the Threshold* and *The Dunwich Romance*

ISBN-13: 978-1-940250-02-1
Available at www.bloodboundbooks.net, your local bookstore or favorite webstore. Also in e-book formats!